START TALKING . . .

Slocum looked at her, dumbstruck. He was about to question her further when he heard furtive footsteps behind him. Before he could turn he felt something hard dig into his back.

Then he heard the click of a hammer cocking.

Slocum's blood froze as Amy Nichols looked at him helplessly, her eyes wide with fear, crackling with warning.

Slocum felt the gunbarrel bore into the small of his back.

"Mister, you better have a good reason for being here," said the voice behind him, "or you won't be here long."

OTHER BOOKS BY JAKE LOGAN

JAKE LOGAN

SIXGUNS AT SILVERADO

B

BERKLEY BOOKS, NEW YORK

SIXGUNS AT SILVERADO

A Berkley Book/published by arrangement with
the author

PRINTING HISTORY
Berkley edition/November 1987

ISBN: 0-425-10347-1

A BERKLEY BOOK ® TM 757,375
Berkley Books are published by The Berkley Publishing Group,
200 Madison Avenue, New York, N.Y. 10016.
The name "BERKLEY" and the "B" logo
are trademarks belonging to Berkley Publishing Corporation

PRINTED IN THE UNITED STATES OF AMERICA.

10   9   8   7   6   5   4   3   2   1

1

John Slocum saw the signs too late.

White thunderheads billowed over the craggy high peaks, swelled over the horizon, and blotted out the feeble rays of the sun. The air was thin here, the trail narrow and treacherous. An old sheep trail, he gathered, clear enough to see in good light, but rocky and dim now as the stormclouds darkened, sucked up the last of the sunlight. In the distance, below timberline, he heard the bugle of a bull elk and he knew the herd must be moving out of the high country. A coyote answered the bugle, and others joined in, their high-pitched yaps oddly distorted in the high, thin air.

"Christ!" he muttered, and his green eyes narrowed, hooded to slits in his wide, rugged face. His jawline tightened, and he reached back of his cantle to the thongs tying down his sheepskin jacket and bedroll. He had two choices, he knew. He could seek shelter and hole up during the storm, or he could follow the switchbacks of the trail down to a lower elevation. He would have a better chance of survival below timberline. Here he was in the open, exposed to the winds that even now gusted through the scrub, blew his sorrel's mane into tangles, sprayed his face with cold dashes of air.

He looked around as his fingers worked at the knots in the thongs. He shivered inside his woolen shirt beneath his worn chaps and denim trousers.

1

There was nothing but bare flat rock all around him. He figured he was at thirteen thousand feet or better, about as high as a man could get and still breathe. He had awakened with a headache this morning, right at timberline, and it had not gone away until he had drunk black coffee, saddled the sorrel, Blaze, so named for its swatch of white from topknot to nose.

The headache was centered at the base of his skull, at the back of his neck. It felt as if someone had driven a maul into the top of his spine. High altitude. Dangerous. A man could get sick, die. He drank coffee and plenty of water, moved slow. Now the headache was gone, but another one, figurative, stood in its place.

He was in a hell of a spot. Each small range in the Rockies had its own weather system. He had been rained on nearly every day since leaving the foothills, but these were snowclouds looming over him, pendulous as elephants, gray and black and full of moisture.

"Shit," he said, touching rowels to Blaze's flanks. The horse picked up a gait, moved across the tundra-like surface, bald above timberline. There was no choice now. He would have to ride off this crest, get into the timber, build a fire, cut some fir boughs for shelter. If he could. He was a good half hour's ride to the edge and he had no idea what was on the other side of the dropoff.

Death, maybe, he mused.

He shook off the thought. That was the first warning sign of panic. When you began to think of death as an allurement, as something that might overtake you, that was the beginning of giving up, of letting your guard down. Slocum knew. He had been to the door before. Death's door.

He shook loose the sheepskin coat, lay it across his

lap as he retied the thongs around his bedroll. Skimpy enough, as it was—a single woolen blanket, an oiled tarp. The cold shivered him then, as an icy gust of wind blew off the rimrock, tore at him with searching, frozen fingers.

Slocum did not halt the horse as he slipped into his jacket and slid the elkhorn buttons through the slitted holes. He turned the collar up and bent his hatbrim to shield his face. The wind felt like sandpaper rubbing against the exposed flesh, like a razor going over two-day stubble without any soap suds.

The jacket helped in the quartering wind. He had a ways to go before he reached the edge of the bald. He had never seen snow in Georgia, before the War. He had seen it in Kansas, though, and in Nebraska, but it was not like the snow in the Rockies, like the deep deadly drifting snow of the Yellowstone or the Powder.

He felt something crinkle in his pocket as he searched for his gloves. He would need those, he reckoned, if he wanted to get out of this with two good hands. He fished out the crude map, unfolded it over the saddlehorn. He quickly noted the landmarks, the faint etchings of the trail he was now on. Silverado could not be more than ten or fifteen miles away. Ten or so hard miles from the looks of it. In this country, that could mean a day's ride or more. Half a day in good weather, maybe.

He refolded the map just as the first few flakes blew down on him. He found his gloves in the other pocket of his jacket, wadded up, stiff. He slid them on his hands, felt the warmth of the sheepskin lining on cold hands. The snow was dry, at first, light.

"Maybe it won't be so bad after all," he said aloud,

and his words sounded false to him, like a man whistling in the dark.

The snow flurries increased, blowing now out of the northwest, straight into Slocum's path. The wind was fierce, cutting, icy as river water in the spring runoff. Slocum bent over the horse, tried to shield his face from the frigid blasts. Blaze bowed his neck, fought the bit. The horse wanted to turn backside to the wind, but Slocum held him to the trail. The horse responded well to the rein, but Slocum did not know if the gelding was a good trail horse yet. The proof would come when the snows blotted out all the landmarks, covered up the sheep path they rode.

The winds picked up, swirled, circled, gathered force. Snowflakes danced in the air like confetti at a parade. But, soon, the snow began to stick. The trail dimmed, faded to a white blankness. The gelding walked on through saltbrush and mountain sage toward the rimrock, and Slocum knew it was going to be bad. As the snow thickened, he knew he would have to rely on dead reckoning to reach Silverado, if he ever did. This was not a flurry, but a serious, mean winter snow. The wind would drift the trail until it was impassable, even if he could see it.

"Son of a bitch," he breathed, and his breath was like white smoke that disappeared in the snowfall.

The horse came to the rim and Slocum saw the dark of trees below when the wind cleared a path through the air. The gelding hesitated, tried to turn back. Slocum spurred him hard, felt him buck under the saddle. The animal started its descent, but Slocum reined him to the sidehill, made him follow parallel paths so that they would not slide down to their deaths. He stopped, once, to tighten the chest cinch when he felt the saddle slide, and he kicked Blaze when he swelled up, jerked the leather tight when the horse emptied his lungs and his chest shrank.

The snow tore at his eyes, blinded him, clogged his nostrils as the wind picked up its velocity. Slocum knew that he was in a full-fledged blizzard. The wind was fierce, driving. The drifts began to pile up, and he rode around them, the horse skittery on the slick slope, fearful of its precarious footing. Once, Blaze went down on one knee and Slocum had to lean back over the cantle to keep from being thrown.

They made the timber, and the snow was not so thick there. But the deadfalls lay like giant matchsticks everywhere and the horse began to sweat, its hide glistening with soapy lather. Slocum knew that the animal was sorely taxed and would founder if he did not give him rest. He reined up, slid out of the saddle. Blaze had swelled up that morning when he threw the saddle on, and the belly cinch was still loose. Slocum left it slack for the moment, dug the makings out of his shirt pocket. He built a smoke, lit it with a sulphur match, cupping his hands to keep the flame from blowing out. The match etched the lines on his face, flickered firelight in his green eyes.

"We could be in a hell of a fix," he said aloud, and already knew he had been on the trail too damned long. The morning headache had gone away, but the air was still slight up here. He figured twelve thousand feet or better, still, and a long ride down to a town he had never seen. The trail was still visible, but the forest was doing its best to blot it out. The snow was already sticking here in the trees where it was warmer.

He smoked slowly, enjoying the scratch of the harsh fumes in his lungs, the lift he got from the nicotine. He might regret using that match later on, he reckoned, but the horse needed rest, needed to get oxygen into its lungs. Blaze was breathing hard, coughing as if to chide Slocum for riding him too hard.

Slocum looked at the ground, saw the fresh elk tracks. Some had passed this very spot not long before. There was a bull, at least three cows, two yearlings. Snow was just now beginning to dust their tracks. The tracks showed that the elk had been walking. He could still smell their scent, heavy in the quiet of the woods.

He finished his cigarette, ground it out with his boot heel. He loosened the cinch straps, pulled them up tight. Blaze started to swell again and Slocum punched him in the flank. The belly went down and John pulled the straps hard, looped the end through the cinch-ring, made his knot. He put a boot into the stirrup and grabbed a hank of mane, pulled himself up. He didn't want the gelding turning under him when they went downhill, maybe taking a fall if the saddle slipped. "The fork goes down," he told himself with a wry grin. He had overheard a Mexican *vaquero* say that to a young cowpuncher once when the kid asked him how to stay in the saddle. The Mexican had made an inverted V with his first two fingers to show the boy what he meant.

"The fork goes down, Blaze, you son of a bitch," Slocum said, and laughed as the horse snorted. For all he knew then, it could have been his last laugh.

Before he had gone fifty yards, the wind howled as it blew down from the high peaks and the snow thickened until he could no longer see the trail.

Slocum was lost.

2

When the blizzard hit full force, Slocum knew that he was lost. He no longer had any bearings. There was no trail, very few trees, no landmarks of any kind. Suddenly, everything turned white. Blinding white.

The snow tore at his eyes, stinging them raw, until he had to duck his head and pull his lanyard tight to hold his hat on. The horse stiffened its legs and stood stockstill as the wind shrieked around them, blasting out of the north with a fury that took Slocum's breath away, drove it back into his lungs, whipped it away from his mouth until he gasped for breath. Snow clogged his nostrils, lashed every patch of exposed skin.

A terrible feeling of claustrophobia engulfed him. He felt boxed in, trapped in an alien world with no escape. A sudden fear welled up in him, a momentary panic that made him want to run and scream. But it was only temporary. He fought to regain his wits, his senses. The suddenness of the cold wind and the terrible sheets of snow that fell on him had caught him off guard.

The snow clung to him, but it was no longer wet. It scorched his face and neck, froze to his beard stubble. He knew that if he stayed here he would die. His only chance was to keep moving, yet there was danger in that, too. He might just travel in an endless circle, going nowhere, until he was too exhausted to fight the elements.

John took a quick breath, shook off the chill that gripped him.

He wiped snowflakes from his eyelashes and assessed his situation with the calmness that comes to a man of courage when he knows his life is on the line and if he does not think straight he will die.

"Dead reckoning," he muttered. That was his only chance, slim as it was. He must remember the landmarks that were there before the blizzard descended on him. He must calculate a path that would take him in the direction he wanted to go, and he must not waver or falter. His biggest battle was with himself right now. His senses were askew, tangled up like cotton thread in a briar thicket.

Slocum tried hard to swallow the lump in his throat. He started out, letting the gelding find his own footing, but guiding him gently with the reins, prodding him on with the spurs to criss-cross the mountain. He would have to make his own switchbacks now, judge the terrain by the way the horse listed, since he could see nothing.

"Don't rub me off, boy," he said to Blaze as he felt the crusty bark of a ponderosa pine brush against the sleeve of his jacket.

The horse picked its way over fallen timber, inched down the mountain. When it got too steep, Slocum turned the animal, keeping in mind that he must keep turning back to dead reckoning. For hours he rode like this, blind, fighting down panic whenever the horse's shod hooves would slip on the icy snow. It was dark in the timber, but he knew it was still daylight. The wind howled and shook the trees, dumping clumps of snow down on his hat. The trail drifted and the horse had to take confusing angles in order to pass them by. Soon,

Slocum knew that he had lost his sense of dead reckoning. He was hopelessly lost, perhaps doomed to the long sleep.

Blaze slid off a rock outcropping and Slocum went flying through the air as the animal hit on its side. John struggled to hold onto the reins. If he lost his horse now, he was a dead man.

He felt the rein slide, but he found his legs, followed the animal as it floundered in a deep drift. He heard its grunts, the terrible sound of its breathing. The wind blew even more fiercely then and snow stung his face, raked his eyes with cold fire.

"Whoa, hold on, boy. Steady now."

Slocum followed the slippery leather to the bridle's bit, touched the horse's face and nose as if to reassure himself that he had not lost Blaze in the fall. The horse lay on its side, winded, unable to struggle out of the deep drift that lay below the overhang from which it had lost its footing. Slocum was winded, too, and he crawled along the horse's belly, feeling its forelegs to see if they were broken. They were intact, but ice-cold, packed with snow. He touched the gelding's haunch, checked its rear legs, its ankles. Nothing broken. But he knew that he had to get the horse up or they would never get out. He nestled against the animal's belly, checked the double cinch. The saddle had not slipped. Slocum breathed a sigh of relief. He didn't know if his fingers would work right anymore. Snow had gotten inside his gloves and his hands felt as if they were frozen.

Quickly, John slipped off his gloves, shook them out. He put his cold hands under his armpits, the warmest place on his body besides his crotch, and waited until the feeling returned to the fingers. His gloves were still wet inside, but they would have to do. He thought about building a fire, almost laughed aloud. Even if he could strike a match, he did not know if he could find wood or shelter in the blinding whiteness of the blizzard that swirled about him.

Slocum crawled back to the horse's head, took a wide-legged stance. He grabbed up both reins, pulled on them. The horse balked and did not move.

"Come on, Blaze," Slocum said. He dug in his heels, pulled harder. The horse floundered, struggled to its forelegs. Slocum kept backing up until the horse gathered its hind legs under it, stood on wobbly footing. The wind ebbed for a minute and John saw that the drift was deep and wide. It would do him no good to mount up now. He would have to lead the gelding out of the deep snows and onto a better surface. The wind picked up again and Slocum saw the trees, the looming rock face of the mountain disappear, like smoke.

He circled, started pulling on the reins when he reached the horse's level. Blaze followed him, snorting. Slocum could barely hear him above the whipping blast of the wind. He did not know if the horse had been injured in the fall. The snow was flying too thick and fast to tell if Blaze was limping, or favoring a leg or a foot. But at least the horse was up, and that was a good sign. He was out of the snowdrift and moving.

But where? Had he lost his sense of direction? Could he really trust his dead reckoning anymore? All he could do was follow the slope, hope that he remembered to switch back every few yards. Now he wondered if he could even tell the difference just by feel, by the pull of gravity. Was he going up, down, or just following a straight track? Slocum was giddy and dizzy and disoriented.

He held up, and Blaze walked into him, halted.

"Steady, boy," he said. He ran a hand down both of Blaze's forlegs and hooves. The horse did not wince. He walked around the animal, feeling the flanks, hind legs, and hind hooves for any sign of discomfort or pain. Blaze held fast, did not flinch. "Good boy," said Slocum, but he decided against climbing into the saddle. They might go over the edge of a cliff or the horse might stumble over a fallen tree. Better that Slocum walked ahead and found their way. If he got hurt, the horse could get him out. If Blaze was injured, it was all over.

Grimly, Slocum bent to the wind and forged ahead through the driving snow. He floundered in sudden drifts, crawled over deadfalls, and wallowed through thick brush. He was tired now, staggering, as he switched back, followed an invisible trail in his mind. From far off, he heard a sound. It startled him, but he could not determine its location nor what had made it. His muscles felt leaden. The snow clinging to his sheepskin jacket added pounds to his burden. The cold numbed his mind, sucked out all the heat under his jacket.

He stopped, struggling to breathe. His fingers were nearly frozen. Around him there was nothing but swirling whiteness, the emptiness of a land transformed into a giant white maw that was drawing him deeper and deeper into its treacherous depths.

Then Blaze whickered, and Slocum heard a crash, heard hoofbeats pounding close by. Startled, Slocum felt his heart jump in his chest. Then it was silent.

An elk, he decided. He thought he had seen something dark bound away, but he couldn't be sure. Everything was so blinding white and he could barely make out the branches of a spruce tree nearby, its limbs clotted with snow, drooping down under the weight.

"Follow the elk," he mumbled, his brain scattering the cobwebs like a woman's broom. He turned, headed downhill, toward the place he thought he had seen the animal. He crouched, searched the new-fallen snow for sign. There was a track, filling in so fast he almost missed it. And another, this one clearly defined, cut into the mud beneath the snow where it had not drifted.

Elated, Slocum followed the track, stooping until he thought his back would break. The elk angled off, following the natural contour of the slope, taking the easiest path. It was slow going, but he knew that the elk was seeking lower ground, leaving the high country for the winter. It was his only chance, at this point. Follow the elk.

The tracks played out as he fell farther behind. The elk, however, was no longer running, but walking fast at a gait that Slocum and his mount could not match. Still, he knew he had gained ground. He was no warmer than before, and there was no let-up in the blizzard's murderous strength, but he felt warmer and his hopes had soared. He tried to find the track, but after a few wide-ranging circles he gave it up. He stopped, looked at his own disappearing tracks in the snow, and slumped into a depression. He became even more disoriented than before, and when he looked at the white, ghostly figure of Blaze, he wondered if it was worth it to go on, to fight against overwhelming odds when all he wanted to do was lie down and sleep, though he knew he would never awaken.

The horse whickered again, jolting Slocum out of his gloomy reverie. He saw Blaze quarter and flick his ears as he shifted his weight. The horse was looking into a swirling mass of powder, but his nostrils were quivering with fresh scent.

"What is it, boy?" Slocum asked, his voice sounding strangely far-off as the wind snatched the sound away.

The animal nickered softly, and Slocum looked down the slope. He saw the dark shapes moving in pairs and threes, small bunches. There were yearlings and cows and big-racked bulls, a herd of elk migrating to the lowlands.

Slocum started counting them, then stopped when he reached eight-five. Still they came, out of the swirling whiteness, their shaggy hulks flocked with snow, their rumps almost invisible. Slocum wanted to jump, to shout, but he quelled the impulse and waited, watching the slow, flowing procession of elk. He knew now that he would find a way down, perhaps even find the trail to Silverado. The elk would take the easiest path, and that meant old sheep trails or woodcutters' trails.

Slocum mounted Blaze, fell in behind the herd. They were easy to follow. The huge herd had chewed up the snow, thrown dark mud atop the drifts. The elk did not spook, but strode at a good clip down the mountain. The snow seemed to ebb and flow now, the gusting wind seemed to lose its force. It was still colder than billy hell, but Slocum no longer felt defeated. The elk trail was wide and deep. Even his horse seemed to walk better, faster.

The elk came to a meadow that was dusted with six inches of snow. Slocum saw it clearly when the wind died, and he saw more than a hundred animals strung out across it. There were many bulls, some with huge racks that bobbed regally as they walked with that peculiar ground-eating gait. Some of the cows glanced back at him and made mewling sounds, but the herd did not bolt. The snow continued to fall, but gradually the wind weakened.

He was halfway across the mountain meadow when he saw it.

The wind stopped howling and through the gauze of dwindling snow he saw the dark shape at the upper edge of the bowl. Before he could fully identify what it was, a great gust of wind boomed out of nowhere and blasted him with a mighty flurry of driven snow.

He wondered, for a moment, if he had imagined it. Maybe, he thought, he was seeing things. Certainly he was weak from the exertion, addled from the freezing cold, but he was certain that he had seen something that was not natural, something man-made.

He waited, as the elk herd pulled farther and farther away from him, bound for the forest fringe beyond, and the wind died down again. He saw the cabin, then, just on the upper edge of the meadow, and smoke curling up from a chimney. He cupped his hands and blew into them, then turned the horse.

He rode toward the square shape, saw it grow larger as he glimpsed it between savage gusts of blowing snow. It was definitely a cabin, made of logs, and the smoke from the chimney was real enough.

"Damn," said Slocum. "We lucked into it, boy. Drew into a straight flush and made it."

The drifts were deep, and Blaze's strength was ebbing fast, Slocum knew. The wind picked up and it seemed sometimes that they were being blown backward. The cabin appeared and disappeared like a mirage, but he knew it was still there. In between gusts, he could smell the smoke and his heart beat faster as he bowed his head and struggled against the brunt of the wind.

Slocum knew a man could die in a blizzard. A man could die within fifty yards of shelter. Within fifty feet. He was not out of it yet, not by a long shot. The snow drifted deep out in the open where he rode, and if there was a trail, it was six feet down or better. Blaze floundered and chuffed, his sides heaving with the strain of slogging through the high drifts.

Slocum dismounted, fought the wind and blinding snow, as he struggled to keep his bearings. The cabin disappeared, then reappeared again. His every breath now tore at his lungs, seared them with icy fire. He stumbled, fell, came up wet and flocked with snow. The cold seeped through his coat, numbed his bones, set his teeth to chattering like a cigar box full of Mexican jumping beans. The cold closed in on him, chilling him to the core and he knew he would soon lose his senses if he did not reach shelter and warm himself by a fire.

He wandered in a half-circle, away from the dark block that he took to be a cabin. Cursing, muttering incoherently, he changed course, leaned into the wind, and forged ahead. His knees turned wobbly on him, and he no longer felt the pain in his frozen feet. He felt as if he were walking on wooden stumps attached to lead weights.

"Keep goin'," he said. "Just keep on a-goin'." And he thought of warm Georgia nights and campfires on lonesome prairie trails, the dry heat of Arizona days and the balmy summer afternoons in Missouri. He kept on going, floundering and wading through belt-high drifts.

He saw the cabin again, closer, but now at a different angle. He had circled, come up almost behind it. He saw something else, too: a lean-to made out of logs. He heard the startled bray of a mule, the distorted, wavery whinny of a horse. And there, under an overhang of rock, there was the lee he had been looking for, shelter from the punishing storm.

Slocum staggered toward the lean-to, dragged Blaze into it, out of the mean howl of the wind. He made out the shapes of two animals and lunged toward them, half-crazed, frozen nearly clean through. The chunky pony whickered and sidled away from him, its eyes rolling wildly in their sockets. A short distance away, a brown, moth-eaten mule munched on grain, eyed him with suspicion. There was room for Blaze in the lean-to, and Slocum led him to a hitchpost over a feed bin. Blaze snorted, drove his head into the trough, nibbled at bits of corn and cracked wheat.

Slocum worked at the cinches with the frozen pegs of his fingers, managed to loosen them and slide the saddle off Blaze's back. He wrapped a rein around the hitch rail, dragged the saddle off to a sidewall. He found an open grain sack inside a barrel, filled his hat. He poured the grain inside the feed bin, blew on cold fingers.

"Got to be folks in that cabin," he muttered, flapping his arms against his sides to drive the chill from his body. Half-crazed, he stomped his feet until the pain returned. The shelter reeked of corn, barley, oats, musty wheat, the acrid tang of a salt lick, leather and manure. He leaned against the sidewall, listened to the wind shriek as it whipped from the rock overhang. "Got to be a fire in that cabin, too," he said to the animals. He laughed insanely and wondered if he should just crawl into a corner and go to sleep. He peered out at the dim outline of the cabin, sniffed the smoke once again, and cleared his head.

"Must be forty, fifty yards away," he said to himself.

He hesitated, wondering if he had the strength to go fifty more yards.

"Hello, the house!" he shouted, his voice hoarse and scratchy, alien to his ears. "Anybody home?"

The wind snatched his words away and he knew that no one could hear him. The animals fidgeted, banged against the log stalls, made low sounds in their throats. Slocum knew that if he waited much longer, he would never make it to the cabin.

He lurched out from under the lean-to and flopped on snow-sodden boots toward the cabin, delirious, dehydrated from the wind, calling out to whomever was inside: "Open the door. I got to get to a fire! Hey, you in the cabin! Open up!"

He fell against the back door, pounded on it weakly. He broke down, weeping.

"Goddamn you, open this door!"

It seemed an eternity before the door opened and he felt a rush of warm air flow over his face. An apparition appeared before him, a dark figure, swimming in the mist of his tears.

"Who are you?" The voice seemed to be coming from the dark shape before him, but Slocum could not be sure. "Where's my pa?"

The voice was high-pitched, strangely eerie in the roar of the wind.

"The name's S-S-Slocum," he stuttered. "John Slocum. For God's sake, man, let me in. I'm near froze to d-d-death."

"Did you kill him, then?"

Slocum heard the shriek above the wind, felt the lash of the person's accusation.

"Damn it, man, let me in. I—I didn't kill anybody!"

A fierce gust of wind slammed Slocum in the back. He pitched forward onto the step. The person in the doorway stumbled backward, knocked off-balance by the powerful force of the wind. Strangling, Slocum struggled to rise from the snow on the step, but the wind pinned him down. He felt the terrible smothering of the suffocating snow and his mind screamed in rebellion. But there was no sound from his throat. He flailed his arms, trying to draw air into his lungs.

Then everything turned black.

3

Slocum opened his eyes, blinked in the harsh glow of the firelight. He had no idea where he was, but through slitted eyelids, he saw flames dancing in a stone fireplace. He smelled the burning wood, heard the wood crackle, saw sparks fly up the chimney. He wasn't in hell, but he knew he had come close to it. His mind was still numb, his body chilled to the bone. He shivered, realized he had a blanket thrown over him. He sat up, looked around.

A trail of snow, melting now in the heat, led to his position and he knew that whoever had brought him in had dragged him to this spot in front of the fire. Probably had saved his life.

The fire drove the cold deeper inside him, made his vision blur, scrambled his brains. His teeth chattered and he couldn't stop them. Somewhere, inside the cabin, he heard disembodied noises, but he couldn't connect them with anything sane or rational. He scrooched closer to the fire, hugged the blanket tighter around him. Still, he felt cold inside and the heat was only something he could feel on his face, not in his bones.

He huddled by the fire, bent over like an aged man, closed his eyes, and fought the pain that stung his toes, his fingers and hands. As he warmed up, a layer at a time, the nearly-frozen parts of him hurt with a ferocious agony that brought tears to his eyes. He wondered how much longer he could have lasted outside, exposed to the elements. Not long, he knew. He felt now as if he would never recover. The pain in his fingers made him want to take a hatchet and cut them off. His feet throbbed until he thought they would burst when they thawed clear through.

She came into the room, but he was hardly aware of her. She squatted in front of him, held out a steaming bowl of liquid that he could not identify. His sense of smell was all but gone, overwhelmed by the agony in his extremities. He couldn't control the shakes as she held out a ladle to him, brought it close to his lips. He saw her as a blur, a faceless person with long hair who was probably female.

"Come," she said, "drink this. You're very cold inside. This will warm you."

He couldn't control the shakes. His teeth sounded like galloping dice rattling in a tin cup. He opened his mouth, tried to drink the hot broth. Some of it entered his mouth, the rest drooled down the corners of his mouth, dripped onto the blanket.

"That's good," she said, and her voice was soothing and low in her throat. She dipped the ladle into the bowl again, pushed it against his lips. His teeth clattered together. He bent his head back, opened his mouth. She poured the broth into his mouth and he swallowed, with effort. "You must have more of this good broth inside you," she said.

"N-no, I c-c-can't," he said, shivering uncontrollably. "I—I'm so c-c-cold."

"I know. My name's Jezebel. Do you understand?"

Slocum nodded, shook all over with the terrible chill

that gripped him, would not turn loose of him.

"You must get something warm inside you. This is very dangerous for you right now."

"C-c-cold," he stammered.

"I know. Please, let me try to feed you." She moved close to him, put an arm around his neck. She set the bowl down, dipped the ladle in, and brought it to his mouth once again. With her left hand, she pried his mouth apart, held it open. "Don't bite me," she said, ladling more of the broth into his mouth. It was not hot enough to scald his tongue, but it was warm. He could feel the warmth in his mouth, but not in his belly. He felt it slide down his throat and turn cold. He gagged and doubled over. Jezebel lost her grip on his mouth and dropped the ladle. It clattered to the floor.

She felt his hands, then reached inside his shirt, touched his chest and belly.

"You're ice cold," she said. "I don't think the broth will do you much good until we can get you warm. What's your name?"

"J-J-John S-S-Slocum."

"Wait here. Try to get warm. I'll be back." He looked at her as she got up, saw a comely young woman with long dark hair, a rounded face devoid of rouge, full lips, a straight, regal nose, startling blue eyes. Her breasts pushed against the bodice of her plain dress, a dress that clung to her body like silk, failed to hide the curves of her hips, the shapely contours of her legs. He watched her go, her buttocks bouncing as she glided across the room to the hall doorway. Then she was gone, and Slocum began to tremble and tears flooded his eyes as the pain in his fingers and toes intensified.

* * *

Jezebel, a stately, yet earthy young woman of twenty-four, had learned to be self-sufficient during the years she grew up with her father, Ebenezer Lee, a prospector. Her mother had died when she was ten, and she was forced to assume the responsibility for maintaining a home for Eb. After his wife, Eliza Lee, died, he became a solitary man and, without realizing it, he had forced Jezebel into the same kind of life. She was the son he never had, the wife who was no longer there. She was the companion at supper and before bedtime. She was his partner in his eternal search for ore, for gold and silver. The years had passed and Jezebel had nursed him through hard times without ever complaining. He had overlooked the fact that she had grown up before his eyes and become of eligible age and was in need of friends her own age. He had tutored her himself, some in books, but mostly in geology and mule-packing, horseback riding, and hunting.

Jezebel accepted her fate because she loved her father and believed in him. He was everything to her and she never entertained the thought of leaving him until he took another woman into his household. She did not press him on this, but listened patiently to his dreams and ambitions and bolstered his confidence whenever he faltered.

Eb Lee was long overdue. She had expected him to come back from a prospecting trek five days before. As the time went on, she grew more anxious and imagined all sorts of terrible things that might have happened to him. Indeed, when the man who called himself Slocum had come to her back door, she thought he had killed Eb and had come to kill her. The storm had frightened her, because she knew no man could stay alive in it, and then when she saw the apparition outside, she was on the verge of hysteria. Now she did not know what to think, but she had seen men die of cold before, and this one was close to it if he did not get warm fast.

She took the bedwarmer with its long, thin handle down from the wall, and opened the gate to the wood stove. She took a pair of tongs hanging from the side of the stove, opened the lid to the bedwarmer's pan-box. She picked out hot coals, filled the pan, then closed the lid. She replaced the tongs and banged the door to the stove closed.

Her bedroom was chill from the cold, even though she had left the door open. She turned down the bed-covers and slid the warming pan between the blankets and sheets, moving it quickly so it would not scorch the linen and the wool. She did not know if she was doing the right thing, because she did not know Slocum. For all she knew about him, he might have killed her father and gotten caught in the storm on his way back to kill her. Yet there was something about the man that made her think he would not hurt her.

He looked so pitiful, shivering like that, and she knew that he must be in terrible pain. She had been frostbitten herself, and once a man who took up with her father got caught in a storm, froze near to death, and died anyway, because he was too far gone for any fire to warm him back to life.

When the bedsheets and the covers were warm, she folded the blankets back over the linens to keep the heat in and returned to the kitchen. She went to her father's room and opened the chest he kept at the foot of his bed. She withdrew his Army Colt .44 in its holster. It was loaded and capped, as always. When Eb was there, he cleaned it once a week to keep it from rusting. When he was gone, she did the same, pushing out the lead balls and dumping the powder, washing the cylinder and barrel in hot soapy water, drying it in the woodstove's oven, then reassembling it and reloading it after exploding ignition caps on each nipple and cylinder.

She put the .44 under her pillow, checked the room one last time, and sighed deeply.

"God, I hope I won't be sorry for this," she said.

Slocum lay on his side, curled up in a ball, shivering. His teeth clacked together rapidly.

"Oh, my," said Jezebel as she knelt beside him.

She lifted his head, cradled it in her arms. She breathed on his closed eyelids. They fluttered. Slocum's hands were cold as death, and her heart pounded as she realized that she might not be able to save his life even by such a drastic measure as taking the man to her bed.

"John. John Slocum. You must get up and come with me. Come to bed. I'll keep you warm."

His eyes opened, then closed again. She slapped his face.

"I've got to get you warm. Can you stand up? Please, you're very heavy. You only have to walk a little ways. John, can you understand me?"

He nodded. She pulled on one arm, tried to lift him to a sitting position. He was heavy. She tried again, bracing herself on widespread legs, pulling as hard as she could.

"You can do it, John. Try real hard."

Dimly, Slocum realized the woman was trying to help him. He felt himself going down, down into a dark cold pit and he couldn't get his arms and legs to work right, as if he were underwater and trying to run. He knew what he wanted to do, but he couldn't make himself do it. His mind was in one place, his body in another. The woman kept going in and out of focus. A thought would come into his mind, then go away again before he could grasp it.

"Up," he said aloud, and struggled to get on his feet. His legs were down there, but they were not his legs. They were on someone else's body. "Got to get . . . up." He felt her pulling on him as he pushed off from the floor. One thing at a time, he thought. Move leg. Lift arm. Pull something up. What? Legs? No, that's not right. Body. Yeah. Pull hard.

The room spun as he half-stood on wobbly legs. He felt as if either he or the room was swaying back and forth and around and around. Jezebel steadied him. He could feel that. He knew that if he leaned the wrong way there would be nothing to support him. He would just fall over the edge of something and never come back. He would go down and never get up.

He was moving. Maybe his legs were working or maybe he was riding a pony. He lurched, crashed into a wall, and it was darker here, and colder. He heard his teeth rattle, but they were not his teeth anymore. They were a sound but they had no substance. He could not feel them. He could feel only the cold and it was getting deeper inside him again. The cold's fingers were working into his flesh, probing, pushing toward the life at his center. He tried to say something, but he did not know how to make his tongue move. His lips were numb and fat and dry, burning, when the rest of him was frozen, frozen hard, and freezing still.

Jezebel guided Slocum into her bedroom. She knew he was going through a bad stage. Thawing on the outside, still cold inside. She took his weight on her shoulder, lunged toward the bed dragging the big man somehow. She ducked from underneath him, saw him crash to the bed, senseless.

The woman undressed him quickly as the storm raged outside. The wind beat at the shutters and the chimney whined with the scud and whirl of air and snow. She thought she heard the far-off cry of a wolf, and in the savage wind she heard bells and chimes and unearthly howls. She heard the bugling of a bull elk, the faint echoes as the sound died away, and, too, she heard the yips and yelps of a dozen coyotes and the wail of lost children, the terrible cry of her father caught out in it, caught in the frosty boil of the falling, wind-driven snow, and her heart tugged for this man on the bed, his teeth still chattering and his skin wrinkled with goose-bumps, so big and yet so delicate that he would surely perish if she did not get him warm.

She looked at Slocum's naked body for only a brief moment, then lifted his legs onto the bed, shoved him close to the middle, pulled the covers over him. She slipped out of her dress, stepped out of her shoes and underdrawers, crawled into the bed, and burrowed under the covers.

Her body was warm. She moved close to Slocum, embraced him, snuggled her nakedness up to his, gave him her heat. The wool blankets kept their heat bundled up underneath. She stroked the man's legs, his belly, his chest, his throat. She worked on him, her fingers rubbing him, causing friction, building up the heat he needed so desperately.

"I'm going to make you well, John Slocum," she said, and she heard her voice quaver with emotion.

She wondered, now, as she pressed her naked body against his, if she was not using the man's helplessness as an excuse to satisfy her own hidden desires. For there was stimulation in touching him, an electric, secret excitement in rubbing her hands over his body and her breasts against his back. The nipples hardened and she felt the slight sting of pleasure in their tips each time they brushed against his bare flesh.

She had dreamed of men before, looked at them from a distance, shy and unobserved, when she and her pa were in town. She was half afraid of them, she admitted, because the only ones she had met were either too old, or young and crude, with the glittering eyes of killers. This man seemed like neither. Even as frozen as he was, she could tell that he was different from most men. She touched the bristly hairs of his three-day growth of beard and there was pleasure in the touch. She looked at his face in the lamplight and saw the strength in his jawline, the fearless honesty in his high cheekbones. She had seen his green eyes, and thrilled to their watery depths. It had been like looking at a bottomless lake in a crater she had seen once above timberline. The water was green and still and so deep she had been afraid of falling down the steep slope of the crater and disappearing forever.

She shuddered, not from the cold, but from the wave of emotion that coursed through her, possessed her. She scrooched closer to Slocum, cupped his buttocks in the cradle of her loins, rubbed against them wickedly, like a child experiencing the first stirrings of puberty without understanding what anything meant.

"I give you my warmth," she whispered, and even the sound of her own voice was sensual to her in the stillness of the room.

She wrapped her arms around his waist, and felt

small against him. She kissed him tenderly on his back, felt him twitch. Boldly, she extended her tongue, laved the spot with its tip, traced a circular path. Yes, wicked, she thought, and she pulled her tongue back in her mouth and smiled to herself. Desire flamed between her legs as she rubbed her delicate lips against Slocum's buttocks, and the fire raced through her veins, torched her senses until she gasped for breath.

"I want you, John Slocum," she whispered and she released her grip on his waist and climbed over him until she faced him. She pushed him gently onto his back, and straightened his legs and arms until he was flat.

She looked at him for a long moment, her heart pounding in her temples, her breath coming in quick pants, as the fear in her mounted. She touched his manhood, half-afraid that he would rise up out of sleep and knock her away for this bold invasion of his privacy.

Her fingers closed around his limp sex and triggered a flood of desire between her legs. She felt a spasmic ripple inside her, a rush of warm fluids. She crawled close to him, put her leg atop his, and nestled on his shoulder. She held the forbidden organ in her hand, petrified with fear that she would be discovered, wanting to take her hand away, but unable to move a muscle.

She closed her eyes, struggled for possession of her senses.

Slocum's member began to stiffen in her hand. She squeezed it, involuntarily, startled that it had moved, was growing fat in her palm.

She began to squeeze and stroke it, delighting in her sudden power, the deep probing pleasure it gave her. Her chest rose and fell with her breathing and she snuggled still closer to him, lay a breast against his arm, rubbed the nipple gently up and down as his manhood grew in the warming garden of her hand.

Wicked, she thought. *Wicked Jezebel*.

4

Jezebel's bedroom took on the aura of a shrine, a secret trysting place lit by the glow of the coal-oil lamp, a place of shadows and dark desires. It seemed to her that she had become someone else, the creature of her fantasies, perhaps. She felt as if she was living in a dream of her own making, that she was a goddess, a princess in a fairy tale, with the power to bring a handsome prince back to life.

The desire grew stronger in her as she thought of this man and herself being naked and alone together. She rubbed her loins against Slocum's leg, felt the heat of desire boil in her. She grasped his penis in her hand and squeezed it, stroked it until it sprang up like a thick stalk. She looked at the blue veins bulging on the surface of his organ, marveled at the throbbing power within her grasp.

"John, oh John," she whispered as she began to wallow over him and slide down his side, moving ever nearer to his swollen shaft. She squirmed, writhed with an uncontrollable desire.

She felt the wetness between her legs. The dank aroma of her own musk assailed her nostrils. She could no longer stand the tension, the agonizing itch that demanded release, satisfaction. She crawled atop the sleeping Slocum, straddled him. She trembled with desire and fear. Dare she go any further? She lowered

herself, felt the hard blunt tip of his manhood against
the inside of her thigh. She rose up, fearful, and shuddered a moment with a sudden spasm. Then she sank
back down, bracing herself for what she was about to
do.

She aligned her sex with Slocum's rock-hard stalk,
felt it nestle into the crease. She stroked along its length
slowly, trembling in every fibre of her body. She eased
forward on her knees, wriggled onto the head, then
scooted backward.

She gasped as the head of Slocum's prick flowed
through the portal, between the desire-swollen lips of
her cleft. She shuddered again as the penis rubbed
against the tiny pleasure button tucked inside the folds
of her crease. A powerful surge coursed through her
flesh. The orgasm shook her, wrenched her senses to a
mindless scramble.

"Oooh," she breathed, and let herself down further
until she felt his shaft fill her. She bolted with another
unexpected orgasm and froze until the spasms passed.
Then, slowly, she began to move back and forth, sliding
up and down. Each slow stroke brought her a pleasure
that made her sob, made her flesh quake with an un-
quenchable desire.

The man beneath her stirred. She stiffened, suddenly
afraid that he would awaken.

Slocum floated through the darkness of dream. He shivered in a black river, swam through a warm tunnel, then
plunged back into icy murk. Shadows flitted at the
edges of the rushing waters, streamed back and forth
across the horizon of his sleeping mind like ghostly
fragments of important objects. He tried to grab them,

to hold them in place, but they danced just beyond his reach.

He felt himself rising out of the dank murk of sleep, and became aware that something was happening to him. At first, only brief sensations crowded into his mind, then bits and pieces of his consciousness slowly returned.

He opened his eyes, saw the apparition looming above him. A face, like a dark angel, floated overhead, and he blinked.

For a long moment he thought that he must still be dreaming. Yet, this was a woman's face he saw, and as his focus cleared, he saw naked breasts, smooth skin, shoulders mantled with soft locks of hair. More, he felt her weight atop him, and his penis buried in the warmth of her sex.

"Jezebel?" he husked.

"Y-yes," she stammered.

He remembered some of it. The cold, the fire, the woman. But not this. Not this naked woman making love to him.

"What's going on?" he asked, his mind still foggy.

"Are you angry? You were so cold and I thought you were going to die. I—I brought you to my bed, and took your clothes off. I knew you had to get warm quick, so I came to bed with you. I—I couldn't help myself, John. I—I've never been so close to a man before. I've never slept with one, never seen one all naked."

"Damn," he said.

"Are you real mad at me?"

"Lady, you took me in all stove up and froze up tight. You got me warm and now I see what kind of nurse you are, I'd be real mad if you *stopped* whatever it was you were doing."

"You mean . . . ?"

In reply, Slocum grabbed her arms, drew her to him. He found her lips, kissed her, as he thrust upward with his hips. He sank into her, felt the obstruction inside her. His eyebrows rose in surprise.

"You're a virgin," he said.

"Yes." She blushed, hung her head in shame.

Slocum shook his head.

"Well, I'll be damned," he said. "Maybe you better get on the bottom, girl, and let me take over."

He eased her onto her side, breaking the connection. She turned over on her back. Beneath him, she looked up into his green eyes, and swam with a sudden giddiness.

"Will it hurt?" she whispered.

"Not much, I reckon."

He eased into her, felt her tighten up for a moment, then relax. He plumbed her, striking again the membrane of her maidenhead, backed off, probed again, pushing gently.

She tautened, relaxed as he pulled away. Again and again he taunted the bastion of her maidenhood, weakening it with every thrust. She caught his rhythm, then, began to move her hips in counterpoint to his.

"Take it," she whispered. "Take it away."

"Yes," he husked. He drove into her, felt the slight resistance, then the tearing away of the veil. He lunged deep, stormed past the torn membrane and dove to the core of her sex, to the very mouth of her womb.

She shrieked softly, gripped him with desperate fingers, then bucked with the lightning surge of pleasure. Tears leaked through the cracks in her closed eyelids, streamed down her cheeks.

"Oh, yes," she sobbed. "Oh, John, yes. Thank you, thank you."

Slocum's brain was still fuzzy. He hardly knew the woman, but he recognized quality when he saw it. In his present state, she appeared beautiful. He felt a growing bond between them, possibly because she had saved his life. The fact that she gave herself to him so willingly was frosting on the cake.

Now, he felt no restraints as he pounded into her thighs, probed the mysteries of her new-found womanhood with masculine abandon. Jezebel, for her part, seemed eager to match his ardor as she met his every stroke with boundless enthusiasm. He felt her buck and writhe with orgasm after orgasm, saw the sweat gleam on her soft skin, and the lampglow turned her into a bronze goddess beneath him, wild, wanton, savage.

He took her to the rarest heights and rode with her, plunging through heady atmospheres and exotic vapors. Her musk was thick in his nostrils as he bucked her to the limit, holding on as she thrashed with sudden, violent spasms.

"I'm going to come," he panted, unable to stay the pleasure in his loins.

"Yes, yes," she screamed softly, and he rammed deep inside her, felt her clutch him tightly as his brain exploded, drenched him senses with hot lava.

He fell against her, limp with exhaustion, spent, his skin tingling with exhilaration. She clasped him to her breasts, stroked his broad back with gentle, loving hands.

"Ummm, it felt so good," she whispered into his ear. "You give me much pleasure, John Slocum."

"It was sweet, Jezebel," he husked. "You're a fine woman."

"Yes," she breathed, "I am a woman now. I feel like a woman. I owe you so much."

"You don't owe me a thing," he said softly. "I think maybe you saved my life."

"I know you saved mine," she said, and he heard the sob catch in her throat, felt her tremble beneath him.

She combed out her long hair by the fire. Neither of them could sleep. They had tried it, with the lamp out, but they only found each other's arms again, and the storm raged outside with howling winds that screamed under the eaves and filled the cabin with ghosts.

"I'm worried about my pa, I guess, more than anything," she said.

Slocum looked at her, warmed by the coffee she had made. He was no longer cold inside, but his toes and his fingers ached some, still. His clothes were dry now and the crackling fire helped blot out the sounds of the storm that battered the cabin with fierce gusts of wind that sometimes blew frosty drafts down the chimney, making the fire crackle and spark, startling them.

"Could be he took shelter before the storm broke," he said "Something I would have done if I hadn't been in the open when she hit."

"No, Pa's a man who watches the weather. He might have gone into Silverado, though."

"I'm sure he did."

"But, he'd know I'd be worried." She stopped combing her hair, looked beyond him, as if trying to picture in her mind what might have happened. She looked beautiful, Slocum thought, was beautiful, in her flimsy gown, her breasts barely showing above the lacy bodice. She had taken it out of a trunk. It was not something she wore every night, he gathered. It was pink and silky and clung to her body, almost caressing it in its flow over her curves.

"Tell me about him," said Slocum. "What did you call him? Ed, was it?"

"Eb," she laughed. "Ebenezer Lee. He's a prospector, like many another man in these parts. 'Ceptin' he's better than most. About a month ago, Pa found a vein of silver, rich as could be, between here and Silverado. He staked out his claim, but there was trouble right off."

"How's that?"

"Men began following him, and someone took a shot at him the other day. And he got an offer from a man he doesn't like much. It was a low offer, too, and Pa thought Carberry was just trying to locate his claim and jump it."

"Carberry?"

"Lucius Carberry. He grubstaked Pa, and he was using that to force Pa to sell. Said he couldn't wait for the money. Why, do you know him?"

"No," said Slocum. "But I was on my way to Silverado to meet a friend. He wrote me that Carberry had stolen his silver claim."

"Who's your friend?" she asked.

"Ned Grover. I knew him in the War. Like your pa, he went off prospecting for gold and silver. I guess he got lucky, finally. I just hope I can give him some help."

"I know him . . . *knew* him," she said quietly.

"Knew him? What do you mean?"

"Ned Grover was killed ten days ago. Just after the miners' meeting. Murdered."

5

Slocum felt a sledgehammer blow of regret slam into his gut. It was hard to believe Ned Grover was dead. There was a man who had fought hard battles all throughout the War. He had suffered deprivation and hardship in the years since. He had fought Indians and Yankees, killed grizzly bear and cougar, scrapped in saloons with everything from fists to barrel staves, and now someone had killed him. It didn't seem fair and it didn't seem right. Ned didn't deserve that. Through it all, he had always been a good man, and more, honest as the day was long.

"He was shot in the temple. His hands were tied behind his back," Jezebel told Slocum, so softly he had to strain to hear her.

"Damn."

"Pa and I were terribly upset. Pa, he said it was another of Carberry's doin's."

"There were others?"

Jezebel put her comb down in her lap, swung her hair over one shoulder so that the thick strands hung over her breast, caught the firelight, shimmered like crow's feathers.

"Yes," she said softly. "Not like that. But shot down in cold blood."

"What happened down there in Silverado? How could that be?" he asked.

39

"The miners, they weren't killers, nor gunfighters. They just broke their hearts, like Pa, and they got in deep with Carberry. He staked most of them. If they struck paydirt, he jumped their claims. Pa and Ned Grover, some of the others, they formed a co . . . all—a col—"

"A coalition?"

"Yes. They figured if they all got together, they could stand up against Carberry. And they did, for a time. Carberry backed off, and me and Pa thought the miners had won. Pa was pretty happy about it."

"And then?" asked Slocum.

"Then the gunslingers came in. They worked for Carberry. Next thing you know, anyone who spoke up against Lucius Carberry was shot down. Oh, they made it look like self-defense, but Pa knew what they were doing. Then everyone got scared and the miners all broke up their . . . coalition . . . and only Pa and Ned Grover wouldn't knuckle under."

It looked ugly, Slocum thought. He had seen bullies like Carberry before. But a bunch of miners had no chance against seasoned gunfighters. He didn't want to say it, but if Ned had been killed, it was likely Jezebel had some cause for concern. Ned was no stranger to the gun, and he didn't back down for anyone.

"Well, I'll look into it when the storm breaks," said Slocum. "Meantime, don't worry. Worryin' never helped nobody."

"I do worry, though."

"Best to look on the bright side," he said, knowing she could see through his bluff. She scooted across the floor, fell into his arms. He held her for a long time and then she kissed him and he kissed her back. After that, they could no longer stand it, and he took her into bed.

They made love again as the storm raged even fiercer than before and the cabin creaked with ghosts.

The wind died by morning, but the snows fell thick and the clouds blocked the sun. When they looked out the windows, there was only the blinding white and the gray sky and the emptiness.

Jezebel fixed Slocum a hearty breakfast. He wolfed down biscuits, steak, half a dozen eggs, and half a pot of coffee. Jezebel ate little, and the worry lines deepened around her eyes. Even with the two of them there, the house seemed empty. Neither of them mentioned her father, but when they fed the stock, he saw that she was weeping. He shoveled a path between the cabin and the shed, left her alone with her private thoughts.

In the afternoon, she stood by the front window, looking outside at the birds nibbling on the suet she had hung from the porch rafters. Slocum polished his boots, checked his pistols, a pair of .36 caliber Navy Colts, and his rifle, a Henry .44 – 40. There was plenty of meat in the smokehouse; he had looked it over, taken a roast from the mule deer Jezebel had shot two weeks before, brought it into the house for supper. "In case Pa comes back today," she told him.

"Slocum," she said, turning away from the window. "Come here. I saw something out there." Her voice was thin, taut with apprehension.

Slocum set down his rifle and rag, stalked to the window. "Where?" he asked.

"Look, beyond those aspen. I saw something. Really, I did. That's the way Pa comes. He left that grove of aspen there a-purpose. Said it was a good landmark for when he come home."

Slocum strained his eyes to see through the thick-falling snow. He saw a dark shape in the copse of aspen, but it could have been anything. He felt Jezebel's hand grip his arm tightly, the fingers digging in hard without her knowing it. She seemed stricken with fear as she stood there, immobile, mute as stone. Slocum squinted against the glare of so much white, saw the animal step out from the trees, pick its way toward the cabin.

"It's a horse," he said. "Can't see any rider."

"Where?" she gasped. Then, "Yes, yes, I see it. Oh, John, I'm scared."

Her fingers dug in deeper until he felt sharp pain shoot through muscle. The horse came closer, and it was, indeed, riderless. Slocum said nothing. Together, they stood at the window, watching the dark horse pick its way through the drifts, seemingly in no hurry.

Every so often, the horse would stop, look at the cabin, then back over its shoulder. When it came within a hundred yards of the house, Jezebel released her grip on Slocum's arm and brought her hands to her face.

"Oh, no!" she exclaimed. "It's Pa's horse. That's Blackie out there!"

"Steady now," said Slocum.

She started for the door and he grabbed her, held her back.

"I'll go out," he said. "Let me get my coat. You get dressed, meet me back at the stables. No use both of us freezing to death."

"Yes, yes," she said, on the verge of hysteria. "Hurry, John, please for God's sake, hurry!"

Slocum retrieved his coat from a wall peg, slipped into it. He put on his gloves. Jezebel retreated to the bedroom to get her wrap. He opened the door, stepped into the glacial quiet. The horse nickered as Slocum descended the porch steps.

"Don't spook on me now," Slocum muttered. He began stalking toward the horse, taking his time, making no sudden movements. "Easy, boy, easy."

The horse stopped, perked its ears. Slocum's voice seemed to soothe it. It held steady as he grabbed the trailing reins. He looked the animal over, checked its teeth, the cinches. The horse appeared to be a twelve-year-old gelding, with good wind, sturdy legs. There was no blood on the saddle. The single cinch was slightly loose, but a man could ride without falling off. Slocum led the animal back to the cabin, circled to the stables in the rear. Jezebel was waiting for him, bundled up against the cold.

"John?"

"Looks like his horse got away from him, that's all."

"There's no . . ."

"No blood."

She breathed a sigh of relief. Slocum handed the reins to her, loosened the cinch. He stripped the horse, put the saddle and blanket on a sawhorse. She haltered it, removed the bridle. Blackie whickered for feed and she grained him, rubbed him down. The horse shook, drank water, settled down to feed.

"What do you think?" she asked as they left the lean-to and walked toward the cabin.

"No saddlebags or bedroll. I'd say the horse ran off in the storm, or right after. Hard to tell. No rifle in the sheath."

"He always carried one when he rode. He had saddlebags, too. Oh, John, I don't know what to think."

"Well, if I leave now, I could track him a ways. Do

you know where your pa's claim lies?"

"No, not exactly. I can draw you a map, giving you the general location, but not the specific place."

"That'd help," he said.

Three quarters of an hour later, Slocum was on the track. Jezebel had wanted to come with him, but he had reasoned with her that her father might be afoot, coming in from another direction. He might need help, as Slocum had. She had waved to him from the porch when he rode off, and he wondered then if he would ever see her again.

The tracks led over the shelf and down into rough, snow-drifted country. Blaze seemed in good shape after his rest, and Slocum had no trouble backtracking Eb's horse. The trail was fresh, and from all indications, the horse hadn't left Lee during the storm, but afterwards, sometime this very morning. Slocum had figured that, but hadn't wanted to worry Jezebel over it. She had enough worries as it was.

The trail wound downslope, followed a high ridge, then dropped over to a wide valley. The horse had zig-zagged across it. Snow filled the tracks, but they were still deep enough to see clearly from horseback.

Slocum checked the crude map Jezebel had drawn for him. From what she had told him, the claim was no more than five miles from the cabin, less than three from town. He figured that Silverado was probably just over the next ridge, south of where he now rode, and the claim somewhere along the ridge north of the valley. The land was broken here, with jutted outcroppings, slide ravines, eroded arroyos. The valley was narrow, flared out in the middle, then closed back up again.

The clouds seemed to lighten, and the sun cast a pearly sheen over the new-fallen snow. The tracks veered off to the right, toward the ridge where Jezebel believed her pa's claim to be, and Slocum, instinctively, loosened his rifle in its scabbard. There were pines and spruce stippling the hillside, plenty of cover for an ambusher, and smaller ridges jutting out from the main one, where a man could hide and pick off an approaching rider.

Slocum did not have far to ride. He saw the swirl of dirt and the stains like fading rust dotting the snow at the point of a small ridge. Blaze started to shy off and began sidling in a sidestep to avoid going any further.

Slocum put the bit to the horse and rode up to the spot, drawing his rifle from his scabbard. The snow was roiled with horse tracks, and the rust-stains were blood. John dismounted, the hairs on his neck prickling up in the silence. Blaze snorted, and Slocum jumped half a foot inside his skin.

"Steady down," he growled. He knelt, examined the tracks. He found a spent shell, smelled it. It was a .44–40 cartridge, and still reeked. Four, five hours old, he figured.

There were a man's tracks leading off into the timber. Flecks of dried and frozen blood were still visible. Slocum grunted, climbed back into the saddle. He started to put his rifle back in its scabbard when Blaze spooked. Slocum grabbed for the saddle horn, gripped his rifle tightly to keep from dropping it.

A second later, from high on the ridge, a rifle boomed. The ball fried the air two feet from Slocum's ear. He saw the puff of white smoke, a dark figure, squatting.

For a long moment, Slocum wrestled Blaze under control, and at the end of that instant, he saw the rifle spout flame, heard its ominous crack a split-second later.

And, in that instant, Slocum saw the glittering eyes of Death staring him straight in the face.

6

Slocum drove spurs into Blaze's flanks, felt the horse's muscles bunch up, spring. Rider and horse bounded into the brush as the rifle ball whistled mortally near, thunked into a snowbank.

In the silence that followed the second shot, Slocum moved Blaze deeper into the ravine, with its snow-flocked brush, ermine-lined boulders. He couldn't stay there, he knew. If the bushwhacker got above him, he could just shoot straight down, make Slocum into wolf meat. But it gave him a moment to collect his thoughts, assess his chances for getting away, or getting up behind the shooter.

Neither option seemed likely, however. He was pinned down, on the wrong side of the meadow, the bad side of the ridge. "Same damned place Eb Lee got cornered," he muttered wryly.

Only where was Eb Lee? There were foot tracks leading away from where the horse had bolted. Blood, too. That could mean that Eb had survived, gotten away. Or maybe he was lying dead somewhere nearby. Slocum discounted that possibility. If he was dead, then there would be no reason for his killer to hang around. Unless Slocum had surprised Eb's killer looking for Eb's claim.

There was no use speculating about it now. Slocum's main concern was in getting out of this predicament. He rode out of the brush, circled a point, put another ridge between him and the ambusher. He listened, heard nothing.

Whoever was up there with that rifle was staying pretty quiet. Or moving. The man up there probably knew the country. He could afford to wait. Or he could move along the ridge and come down on top of Slocum. Slocum was in the rainbarrel and there was no way out.

He moved Blaze along the edge of the ravine, hunching low in the saddle. At one point, he stood up in the stirrups, peered over the edge. The rifle on the ridge exploded, and a bullet searched the snow in front of him, kicking up clumps, spattering his face with cold mush. He ducked, his heart pounding like a triphammer.

The rifleman had moved midway down the ridge. He wasn't coming in from above or from the side, but was trying to cut him off!

Slocum rode closer to the mouth of the ravine, and took a stand. He stood up in the stirrups again, brought his rifle up to his shoulder. He poked the barrel over a snowbank and waited for his target to fall into his sights.

Several moments trickled by, like sand in an hourglass. Slocum saw no movement, heard no sound. Uneasy, he blinked his eyes, scanned the snowscape without moving his head. After several nerve-wracking minutes, he rode out of the mouth of the ravine. He stayed low, kept the trees and brush at his back to present no silhouette.

There was no sign of the bushwhacker on the exposed slopes. But, Slocum reasoned, the man could be in the trees, just waiting for him. He rode toward the last spot where he had seen the man, wary, his rifle held in a one-handed firing position.

On the far horizon, he saw the lone rider slapping his sorrel horse, riding into the timber. Seconds later he was gone. Slocum had no doubt that his bushwhacker was that man on the sorrel. He considered riding after him, but he had promised Jezebel he would look for her father, and he wanted to make the remaining daylight count. He rode up the slope, made the top of the ridge an hour later. The snow was laced with horse tracks and boot tracks.

There was more blood, and he found a brass cartridge buried in the snow, another .44–40 from a rimfire Henry, he figured. The boot tracks criss-crossed back and forth over the ridge, then disappeared in thick brush. It would take hours to sort them out. Some tracks were obliterated by wind and slides, but he got the general picture.

A lone bushwhacker had surprised the man on horseback—Eb Lee, Slocum figured. Then Lee had made his escape on foot, traveling upslope, switching back and forth. He had fired his rifle at least twice, probably more. Atop the ridge, he had held the man off for a time, then managed to escape. The sniper had searched for his quarry but had not found him. He was still searching when Slocum had ridden up.

"Eb Lee!" Slocum shouted. "If you're alive up here, I come as a friend. The name's Slocum. Your daughter is safe. I'm riding to Silverado."

His voice was swallowed up in the trees and the whiteness, and probably had not carried far. There was no use searching any longer. Eb Lee didn't know him, might mistake him for a bushwhacker. Slocum had no desire to catch a bullet, Lee's or someone else's. Slowly he picked his way back down the slope, wondering if Lee was somewhere watching him.

He stayed to the open, putting distance between him and any surprise rifle shots. He crossed the valley and found the trail to Silverado. It was only a depressed path under two or three feet of snow, wide enough for a wagon. The sun began to fall away in the west when he rode over the last ridge, saw the ramshackle jumble of buildings below. Blaze whickered at the sight of civilization. The trail here showed fresh tracks, probably where the bushwhacker had ridden back in after leaving the high meadow.

"Well, mister," he muttered to himself, ''I don't know you, but you sure as hell know me.''

The town was built on a flat between two steep canyon walls. It was a crowded, packed cluster of clapboard buildings, false fronts, houses perched precariously on both hillsides scarred by mine openings and snow-covered railings. The streets were clogged with snow, but dozens of men manning shovels had cleared a path down the center of the main one. Shopkeepers loaded snow in wagons hitched to mules, and there were signs that the people had been busy since the storm broke. The snow was grimy with mud and fresh dirt, the air filled with steam from men's breath as they toiled to clear the drifts.

Slocum noticed the signs and posters proclaiming FAIR PLAY FOR MINERS and NO MORE CLAIM JUMPING! Some of these were riddled with bullet holes. Others were smeared with red paint that resembled blood.

Men looked up at Slocum as he rode past, and he read suspicion, distrust, fear, and anger in their faces. He looked at the signs on the false fronts, passed the Silverado Saloon, rode on to the stables at the end of the main street. He rode up to the wide doors and called out. A door opened and a man's face appeared.

"Board?" he asked.

"Yep," said Slocum.

The face disappeared and the double doors swung open. Slocum rode in and dismounted. The stables reeked of sweat, manure, wet hay, and musty grain. The stableman, a balding, stocky man, stepped up as Slocum dismounted, took the reins from the stranger's hand.

"Be a dollar a day, grain fifty cents extry."

"Anybody ride a wet sorrel in here?" Slocum asked, digging in his pocket for greenbacks.

"Mister, you already done asked one question too many."

"Mind if I look around?"

"Suit yourself. It's still a dollar a day, fifty cents extry fer grain."

"I'll pay a day. If I stay over, I'll pay you tomorrow."

"Four of the clock you ain't here, I turn your horse out back and it's six bits a day out yonder in the lot, dollar extry fer feed."

Slocum paid the man and looked in the other stalls. The sorrel horse had been rubbed down. Marks of the curry comb still showed on his hide. The brand on the hip was a Slash B, but it didn't mean anything to Slocum.

"Who owns this sorrel?" Slocum asked.

"Mister, you are a persistent cuss, ain't ye?"

"All I want is a name."

"Wal, now, you must think this is a information bureau. I tell you, son, a mouth like yours is big trouble 'round here. I ain't answerin' no questions. You'd best get your carryin' gear and walk on about your bizness."

Slocum resisted the urge to take a poke at the stableman. He shrugged, drew his rifle out of the scabbard, and untied his saddlebags. He slung those over his shoulder and stalked from the stables. The stableman snorted as he left and Slocum heard the creak of leather as the man loosened the cinch on Blaze's saddle.

He strode to the Silver King Hotel and checked in at the desk. He took a small room for an exorbitant four dollars. The clerk was as sullen as the stablemaster, and Slocum didn't press him much. He put his gear in his room and went back downstairs. He walked up the street to the Silverado Saloon, crossing long shadows that cut the boardwalk, blinking at the glaze of sun on the windows of the barber shop. The air reeked of dirt and snow and sweat. The clunk of shovels against earth and wood and stone mingled with the sounds of men's voices. It wasn't much of a town, he thought, and it was already showing an ugly disposition.

The saloon was in full kick at that hour.

Slocum pushed at the door that was closed against the cold, felt the blast of heat when he entered. Men crowded the bar, sat at oval tables, lolled against the walls studded with the stuffed heads of wild game. The din of conversation died as the tall man cut a path toward the bar. The clink of chips died away, the swick of cards slid into a wary silence as men's eyes fixed on the stranger.

Slocum wedged himself a spot at the long bar, stood with one foot on the brass rail. A spittoon clanged eerily with the accurate spat of tobacco. The barkeep took his time acknowledging Slocum's presence as the conversations rose up again, changed pitch, flowed from growl to mutter to whisper.

"Name your poison," said the barkeep to Slocum.

"Any Pop Skull you got will do," said he.

"Mister, we serve good whiskey here."

"Bring the bottle, then."

"I don't see any money on the bar."

Slocum laid a sawbuck on the counter. The barkeep brought a bottle and a single water-smeared glass. He took the bill, came back with four dollars change. Slocum's eyebrows arched, but he said nothing. He poured himself a drink, took a swallow, then turned his back to the bar.

"I'm looking for anyone who called Ned Grover friend," he bellowed. "I'll buy you a drink in his memory and shake your hand."

The mutters and the whispers switched off to a dead silence. Men stared at him as if he had mentioned the Black Plague.

Slocum stepped away from the bar to the center of the room. He swept the assemblage with a withering glance of his green eyes, and all could see the lone muscle twitching in his cheek. It seemed that his eyes were struck with a hard flint. Some men flinched as if showered by their sparks.

"Ned was my pard," he boomed, "and if he was murdered, I aim to see his killer brought to the mark. If there's law here, the murderer will hang. If there isn't, he'll answer to my sixgun."

No one moved. No one said a word. The silence stretched from one interminable moment to the next. Someone coughed. Another man cleared his throat.

Then a lusty cheer rose up from a cluster of miners, all armed to the teeth, who were sitting in one corner of the saloon. The cheer died as suddenly as it was born.

The hardcases scattered around the room scraped their chairs and looked uncomfortable. Finally one of them rose from his table.

"Mister," he said, "I don't know who in hell you are,

but if you came lookin' for trouble, you done found it."

"And who in hell are you?" asked Slocum.

"Who's askin'?"

"The name's Slocum. John Slocum."

"I'm Herb Unger and I've heard you're a no-good, yellow-backed excuse for Southern trash."

Slocum didn't blink an eyelash. "Well, if you work for Carberry," he said, "tell him John Slocum would like a word with him."

Unger's hand moved toward his pistol. Before his fingers could touch his gunbutt, Slocum had his gun cocked and leveled at the man's belt buckle.

"What'd you do that for?" asked Unger, beginning to shake in his boots.

"I got this pistol from an insurance salesman," said Slocum. "Premiums are all paid up."

"Jesus Christ," cursed Unger.

The silence moved in again as men licked dry lips, avoided looking directly into Slocum's eyes. He slid the pistol back into its holster, hammer down, slick as it had come out.

"I hope that was part of a prayer, Unger," said Slocum. "You may not have much time left."

Unger's jaw jutted out belligerently. His porcine eyes narrowed to slits. He was a burly man, thick-necked, slope-shouldered, who wore his pistol tied low on his leg. He had to lean some to go after it. Slocum wasn't going to tell him any different, but he penalized himself some seconds wearing a rig like that. His hardcase friends looked at Unger, wondering if he was going to open the ball.

"You son...of...a...bitch," Unger said and he

leaned a little farther to one side, flexed the fingers of his shooting hand.

Slocum never moved. He just waited. He waited like the hawk waits, like the wolf when it is sure of its prey.

Everyone in the room knew what he was waiting for.

7

Slocum watched Unger out of the corner of his eye. His glance took in the other hardcases at his table and the tables nearby. None seemed anxious to back their spokesman, but Slocum had no doubt they would try for him if Unger did. He had seen such men before in a hundred towns, in dozens of saloons. They lived by their wits and their guns, but at heart they were cowards.

"Next time I draw," said Slocum evenly, "I shoot."

"You push a man hard, Slocum."

"Seems to me you opened the conversation, Unger."

"Well, I'm closin' it. Come on boys, this damned place stinks of mud rats."

Unger relaxed. The men with him rose up from their chairs and followed him out of the saloon. Slocum watched them go, watched for any hesitation, any sudden twitch. The door opened and closed again when the last man left. The icy chill hung in the air for a few moments until the heat sucked it up.

The miners began laughing, taking drinks.

"Buy Slocum a drink," someone said.

"I'll buy him one," said one galoot. "In honor of Herb Unger's tail what's tucked betwixt his legs."

More laughter.

"I've got a drink," said Slocum. "I still want to buy one for the man who'll tell me about Ned Grover. And, if any of you know Ebenezer Lee, I got some information for you."

At the mention of Eb Lee's name, the miners fell silent for a moment. One of them spoke up.

"Eb Lee's a fool," he said, "but he's man enough to stand up to Carberry."

"What's got you boys buffaloed?" asked Slocum.

The man who had spoken got up from his table and ambled toward Slocum.

"I'll tell you what, Slocum. Carberry's claim jumpin'. Unger and those boys were some of the men who do the dirty work. Carberry runs the town. Some of the miners go along with him. We ain't seen Eb Lee in three weeks, but we hear he's got him a big claim."

"What's your name?" asked Slocum.

"Dan Bladen. I had me a claim, too. Carberry staked me. When he wanted it all, I gave it to him. He had a pistol jammed up against my balls. Hell, I can't buck the man. Neither can nobody here."

"That's right," muttered one man.

"As for your pard, Ned Grover," said Bladen, "we don't know who kilt him, but he's six feet under now and we ain't askin' questions. You want to stay healthy, you'll do the same. Unger backed down today, but he'll carry it with him and put your lights out when you least expect it. Backshooters, that's what they are. You won't even hear the ball a-comin'."

Bladen was a young man, dark-haired, with wild blue eyes, a perpetual sneer to his lips. He seemed to have a chip on his shoulder a foot high. He drank a swig of beer and sat back down at his table. Slocum could see the smouldering anger in him and in the faces of the others who crowded the saloon, drinking away their troubles, frightened of forces beyond their control.

"All right, Bladen," said Slocum. "Thanks. I'll poke around, see what I can find out. If Carberry wants me, he'll know where to find me."

John strode back to the bar and poured himself another drink. He had made little headway, but he had flushed out some of Carberry's men. Maybe one of them had killed Ned. There was so much fear in the room he couldn't cut through it, but Unger would spread the word that Slocum was in town. Carberry would either back off and wait, or he would come gunning for him. Either way, it didn't make much difference. If there was no law here, as it seemed, then Slocum would have to take up that slack.

A man at the bar looked over at Slocum sheepishly.

"You want Carberry," he said, "he'd likely be at the Montana Mining Company. Just down the street. He's generally there until dark or after."

"Thanks," said Slocum. "Obliged."

"Your funeral," said the man, and turned his back to Slocum.

The patrons' voices rose and fell in conversation like the drone of summer insects in a fruit orchard. Slocum looked at the bottle of whiskey in front of him. He had no intention of drinking it all just then, but he felt like it. Next to smallpox, cholera, gunshot wounds, and pneumonia, whiskey was the biggest killer on the frontier. He'd had his brushes with Pop Skull, and there were times when it was good medicine. It could also be used as a bribe in some cases, and he was hoping to attract someone there whose tongue could be loosened to tell him what he needed to know.

"You won't get anyone in here to trust you, Slocum," said a man who came up behind him and stood at his elbow. "Carberry runs this town and the people in it."

Slocum turned around to survey the man. He was startlingly young, but his eyes looked older than God's. He had whiskey in him, and from the dry, cracked lips with which he spoke, he'd been on a long bender. His simple clothes reeked of sweat and dried vomit. He was short of stature, slim, with crackling pale blue eyes, a cut across the bridge of a nose that had been broken at least once.

"You know my name, I don't know yours," said Slocum.

"They call me Whistler. But the name's Douglas. Tom Douglas."

"You know this Carberry?"

"You gonna drink all that whiskey by yourself?"

The man held out a shaking hand. There was an empty tumbler in his fist. Slocum filled it halfway with the whiskey, made room for Douglas at the bar.

The man slipped into the spot next to Slocum. He got half the whiskey down before he choked. For a moment, Slocum thought Douglas was going to die right there. He doubled over, held onto the bar with a grip that turned his knuckles white. His frail body convulsed as choking paroxysms shook him like a rag doll.

As suddenly as the convulsion had come, it was gone. Douglas stood up straight at the bar, wiped his mouth with his shirtsleeve, and steadied like a tree after the wind dies.

"I was staked by Carberry," said Douglas. "One of the first. I run into a vein of silver up the canyon and whooped into town. Lucius bought me a lot of drinks in celebration and next thing I knew he had him a paper with my scratch on it saying he owned the claim."

"Any witnesses?"

"Yeah, Unger and Will Halsey." Douglas laughed

wryly. "Will broke my arm after that. Not my drinkin' arm, the other."

Douglas held up his left arm. It had been broken, and it had not set right. It was crooked when he held it up like that, bent just above the wrist.

"Why don't the miners stand up to Carberry and run him out of town?" Slocum asked.

Douglas swallowed the rest of the whiskey in his glass. This time it didn't choke him. He didn't even blink as the rotgut burned down through his innards.

"Do you know what dread is, mister? I don't mean fear. Fear you can deal with, but dread is like a shadow that follers you all around and you can't shake it. It's like comin' into a dark room at the end of a hard day and you know somebody's in there. You can't see him, but you can damned sure hear his breathing. It's like being out there on the trail and looking back over your shoulder all the time because you know somebody's follering you. 'Cept you shouldn't be lookin' back, but ahead, because the son of a bitch is waitin' for you.

"Well, that's what dread is, and these men dread Carberry. The man has a heart as cold and black as a chunk of anthracite coal. Now, you was askin' about Ebenezer Lee. He's one of those who stands up to Carberry, but nobody's seen him in two, three weeks, and it's well known that he and Lucius had some words. Now, I ain't sayin' Ebenezer's been done in, and I don't know for sure if your pard Ned Grover was kilt by Carberry, but there's so much suspicion in this town you have to wade through it in hip boots."

"I was hoping there might be witnesses."

"Mister, if they was, they'd be plum dead by now."

"I see," said Slocum. "But didn't Ned have any friends? Didn't anyone here give a damn about him?"

"Oh, I reckon he did. Eb was one such. Might be 'nother or two."

"I guess I'll have to go beard the lion in his den," said Slocum.

"You be careful you don't get clawed to death," said Douglas.

Slocum left the bottle and stalked out of the saloon. His boots rattled the sodden boardwalk and slipped on icy wood. He stretched, took in a deep breath of air to clear his head. He hadn't learned much, but he had gotten a couple of men to talk out of turn. First Unger, then Douglas. One thing was certain: The men in Silverado were scared. And they were scared of Lucius Carberry. Slocum had no doubt that there were grounds for their fear.

He walked a few paces, then he heard the door to the saloon open and slam shut. He turned, and saw a man coming his way. He started to step off the boardwalk to let the man pass, but the man slowed, looked around furtively.

"Slocum," he said. "Hold up."

"You want to talk to me?"

"I shore do, son. The name's Dewey Proctor, and we got fat to chew."

Slocum looked the man over. He was short, stocky, and muscular. Powerful shoulders stretched his heavy woolen capote tight. He had the hood down, and his bearded face seemed carved out of mountain granite. The cheekbones were high, the dark brown eyes wide set, deep, the whites laced with red lines. His nose was bulbous, red-tipped from raw winds and the cold. His hair was a thick shock of black curls, salted with gray.

"Why didn't you say something inside the saloon?" Slocum asked.

"Didn't want to say nothin' in front of the others," said Proctor.

"You ready to say something now?" Slocum asked sarcastically.

"Maybe. I could use a friend right now. But I 'spect Unger, or one of his bunch, has got his danged eyeballs a-trackin' us right now."

Slocum looked up and down the street. He didn't see anyone acting suspiciously, but then he couldn't see through walls. Proctor looked around as well, but he showed no sign that anything was amiss.

"Just what did you want to talk to me about, Proctor?" asked Slocum.

"I know where Eb made his big strike a few weeks ago."

Slocum was surprised. He looked at Proctor more closely. The man seemed straight. His voice showed no signs of deception. It was pitched low, just above a whisper, but that was understandable.

"That's interesting," said Slocum. "Even his daughter doesn't know where he staked his claim."

"He was a-goin' to tell Jezebel today. I was supposed to meet Eb just before that big storm hit, but Eb never showed up. I had to turn back. But I reckoned something was wrong. Not like Eb to say he'd be a place and not show up."

"Honest, is he?"

"Eb never went back on his word, long as I've knowed him. He says he's going to meet you at a place, he meets you."

"You think he's dead?" asked Slocum.

"Dead or waylaid, for shore," replied Proctor.

"You may be right." Slocum told him about the riderless horse coming to the cabin, about the tracks, the roiled snow. He didn't say anything about being ambushed. He would keep that to himself for a while, until he knew for sure whether or not he could trust Dewey Proctor.

"Tell me again where you saw the blood and the tracks," said Proctor.

"In that long valley up there, not an hour's ride from town. At the foot of the slope on the east side."

"That ain't far from where me'n Eb was to meet. We'd better try and get on out there. If he lost his horse, he'll be afoot."

"I'm ready," said Slocum.

"Meet you in a hour," said Proctor. "I got to get my gear together. My horse is in the stables. That O.K. with you, Slocum?"

"That'll be fine, Proctor."

Dewey crossed the street and walked toward a hotel down the block. Slocum watched him go. He saw a man step out of the shadows between two buildings and begin to follow Proctor.

Slocum started to warn the miner, but something else caught his attention. Herb Unger stepped out from the same place and looked across the street at Slocum.

Unger held up his right hand, pointed a finger at Slocum. He brought his thumb downward like a pistol hammer. Then he grinned.

Slocum did not grin back. His eyes narrowed. Unger was joined by two other men who had also been waiting in the shadows. They all looked at him ominously, then split up, going their separate ways.

So, there had been at least five men waiting for him to leave the saloon.

Slocum had the uneasy feeling that had he walked

past them, he would now be lying in the street, leaking blood.

Two of the men crossed the street. They seemed in no hurry. The other walked on the same side as Dewey had taken. He also took his time.

Unger went into the store building. Slocum saw the sign on the false front: STEUBEN'S GENERAL STORE, *Karl Steuben, Prop.*

Slocum crossed the street and headed toward the store.

He wasn't finished with Herb Unger yet. Not by a long shot.

He entered the store and looked around. He saw a woman clerk at the back counter, a man standing stacking bolts of cloth on a shelf. There was no sign of Herb Unger, no trace of his ever having entered the store.

Slocum felt his flesh crawl as he stalked to the back counter. He wondered if Unger might be hiding in the store, ready to kill him. The woman at the back looked up at him. She was young and very pretty. Her eyes widened and she flicked them toward the back door.

Slocum looked at the door and saw that it was still moving.

He heard another door slam, and knew without being told that Herb Unger had walked straight through and out the back.

Slocum stopped at the counter and looked hard at the girl.

"Everyone knows you are here," she whispered, "and why."

"Herb Unger go out the back way?"

"Yes," she hissed.

"You a friend of his?"

"N-no," she stammered. "Slocum, I'm Amy Nichols, and I saw Ned Grover murdered."

Slocum looked at her, dumbstruck. He was about to question her further when he heard furtive footsteps behind him. Before he could turn he felt something hard dig into his back.

Then he heard the click of a hammer cocking.

Slocum's blood froze as Amy Nichols looked at him helplessly, her eyes wide with fear, crackling with warning.

8

Slocum felt the gunbarrel bore into the small of his back.

"Mister, you better have a goot reason for being here," said the voice behind him, "or you won't be here long."

"I came in here to buy a pair of gloves and some wool socks," said Slocum evenly.

"Miss Nichols, show the gentleman what he wants."

Slocum felt the pressure in his back ease, then go away as the pistol was withdrawn. He turned and looked into the steady eyes of Karl Steuben. Steuben had thick eyebrows jutting over muddy blue eyes, a massive walrus moustache that framed a square jaw and drooped over a weak mouth. He wore denims, an apron, and the converted Colt's dragoon in his hand looked like a miniature cannon.

"You treat all your customers this way?" said Slocum.

"Vell, I heard about you, Slocum. You come to town looking for trouble." Steuben had the faintest trace of a German accent. He stood a head shorter than Slocum, his dark hair slicked down with pomade and parted in the middle.

"A man came through here a minute ago. I just wanted to talk to him. Herb Unger. Know him?"

"Ya, I know Herb. I don't know you."

"Maybe you know Lucius Carberry, too."

"Humph!" snorted Steuben. "You buy your goods and be on your vay, Slocum. I vant no trouble in my store."

Slocum said nothing. Steuben moved away, but he kept a wary eye on the stranger. Amy Nichols returned with several pairs of gloves and some woolen socks.

"I—I can't talk now," she whispered, "but if you meet me after store hours at Mrs. Willoughby's boarding house, I can tell you what I know."

"I can't make it definite," said Slocum.

"Any time," she said sweetly, smiling up at him. Steuben, a few aisles away, cleared his throat.

"Looks like Steuben's on the wrong side," he said.

"Shhh!" Amy showed him the leather gloves, some lined with sheepskin, others with moleskin. She was an attractive young woman, with short dark hair, eyes the color of hazel nuts, pert breasts that kept her bodice taut, a small waist, and comely hips.

Slocum bought a pair of gloves and two pairs of socks.

"You married?" he asked.

"No," she said, and blushed. "You shouldn't ask such things."

"There's other things I could ask," he said.

"Are you finished there, Miss Nichols?" barked Steuben.

"Yes, sir," she said, and the crimson still flowered on her cheeks. "You must go, Mr. Slocum," she said under her breath.

"Well, thank you very much, Miss," he said loudly. "Goodbye."

"Goodbye," she husked.

Slocum passed close to Steuben as he left the store.

"Steuben, next time you draw on me, you'd better be prepared to shoot."

"Och? And vy is this?" asked the German shop-keeper.

"Because I'll blow your head off if you even look cross-eyed at me again. So long, Steuben."

He could hear the man swearing in German, the soft wrinkled stream of Amy's laughter as Slocum walked outside.

Lucius Carberry chewed the stub of the cigar to shreds, spat out chunks of sodden tobacco that tinked against the brass spittoon on the floor. He hunched over his massive desk like a gargoyle guarding a granite build-ing, his smoky blue eyes narrowed to angry slits. He was a beefy man only in his hands and arms, built like a pugilist, with wide shoulders, narrow hips, and strong, lean legs. His blond hair was cropped at the neck and sideburns, slicked down with scented water, combed straight back from his wide forehead. He had lips like a woman's, soft and squishy, pouty, ever wet from the cigar, from the constant lick of his tongue.

"You dumb son of a bitch," he spat, and squibs of tobacco stuck to Unger's coat, splattered his face.

"Hell, I didn't know who the bastard was," said Herb. "He outdrew me and I figured it wasn't my time, so I backed off."

"He's the one Grover said was coming."

"I know that now, Lucius. Christ. He had me cold."

Carberry slammed back against his chair, threw the ragged butt of the cigar down at the spittoon with vio-lent force.

"No, Herb, *you* had *him* cold. Up there in the valley. You should have put out his lamp then."

"Shit, I tried. Tried until my hands froze so's I couldn't work 'em."

"Well, it cost you, didn't it? Now you have to face him down."

"Hell, that man's pure trouble, Lucius. Take more'n one of us to bring him down."

"He's no different than anyone else," said Carberry. "He's just got you buffaloed."

"Maybe so. I like to know what kind of man I'm facin'."

"Now you know. I don't want any more excuses. You do whatever you have to do, use as many men as you need, but I don't want Slocum pokin' around in my business, hear?"

"I hear, boss," Unger said sarcastically. "I think he's going to help us, matter of fact."

"Oh? How?" Carberry's face was red. It looked like a bomb ready to explode.

"Well, look, I saw him a-talkin' to Proctor. Those two are up to somethin'. Proctor and Lee are thick as fleas on a redbone's back. I figger they're aimin' to hook up with Lee."

"Well, that bastard Lee hasn't filed on his claim yet, not legal, anyways. As long as he's got friends and kin, I'd have trouble filing against it. Better to put him under once we find his claim," Carberry said.

"I know. We're tryin'. He don't go the same ways twice, and ever' time we get close, he goes to ground like a damned rabbit. Feller knows those hills like the palm of his hand."

"Yeah," Lucius admitted. "That's one reason I staked him. The man can read rock. Likely his'll prove out the richest claim we got."

Unger pulled out the makings, began building a

smoke. His forehead knitted in thought. Carberry picked up a pewter paperweight and began toying with it. Unger struck a match and lit his quirly. He blew a plume of blue-gray smoke into the air.

"Best place to get Slocum," said Unger, "would be here in town. We can put three, four guns on him, blow his lamp plumb out when he least expects it."

"No, that won't do," said Carberry. "You only push these hardrock miners so far. You do an open killing in town and we'd have a lynch mob buying hemp. You follow this jasper. He leaves town, you get on his track, put some holes in him. No witnesses. If Proctor gets in the way, shoot him."

"Slocum asked a lot of questions about Grover," said Unger, his breath laced with smoke.

"Yeah?"

"Nobody answered him."

"Nobody knows," said Carberry. "Except . . ."

"Except what?"

"Nothing, maybe. But that gal of his, Amy . . . she don't look right to me."

"Steuben'll keep her in line," said Unger.

"I don't trust him, either," said Carberry. "I pay him good, but he ain't none too comfortable being a spy for Montana Mining."

"Hell, long as you keep him in green and silver, he'll toe the mark."

"We'll see," said Carberry. "You better go on now. I want to do some hard thinkin'. You stay with this Slocum. He knew you shot at him?"

"Not so far's I know," Unger said. He drew deeply on the cigarette.

"Yeah, well, we don't know *what* he knows. If you get him and Eb Lee, you know what comes next."

"Yeah," said Unger, grinning. "We got to take his next of kin down, too."

"A shame," Carberry mused, fondling the paper-weight. "She's a right purty gal."

Unger grinned again, touched a finger to the brim of his hat. In a moment he was gone. Carberry let the paperweight fall from his hand. It hit the desk with a thunk that sounded like the trapdoor springing on a gallows.

Slocum ate a hurried plate of steak and beans and washed it down with strong coffee at Ike's Cafe on Main Street, then went back to his hotel for his gear. The sun was setting by the time he arrived at the stables. This was a hell of a time to track a man, he thought, but he welcomed the oncoming darkness. The dark made things simple. The town was quieting down, and every sound was amplified. Lighted lamps illumined the windows of the establishments that were open, and the street was almost emptied of people.

The stableman was putting out feed by lamplight when Slocum strode through the door, his boots scuffling through the damp straw. Proctor was already there.

"You ready?" he whispered, when Slocum came close.

"This a good time to be riding out?" Slocum asked. "It's going to be pitch black after a while."

"Me and Eb had an agreement," Proctor said, his voice still hushed. "Tell you about it when we get out of here."

Slocum put his saddlebags and rifle down, and walked to the stall where he had seen the sorrel. Puzzled, Proctor followed him. The stableman was in the stall. He snorted when he saw Slocum.

"What is it, Slocum?" asked Proctor.

"That sorrel gelding there. Know who rides it?"

"Yeah. That's Herb Unger's horse. How come?"

"I saw that horse this morning. Its rider took a couple of potshots at me."

Proctor put his fingers up to his lips in a gesture for silence. Slocum nodded. The stableman came out of the stall, an empty tin in his hand.

"Your horse has been curried and grained," he said to Slocum.

"And you've been paid for it," Slocum said.

"Jake," said Proctor, "this here's John Slocum."

"I know who he is. He talks too goddamned much."

"John, this is Jake Wheeler. He hates everybody. Human, that is. He gets along with horses and mules jest fine."

Proctor laughed, but the stableman didn't.

"If only that sorrel could talk, eh, Jake?" said Slocum.

"Horses know better, Slocum. And, Dewey," he said to Proctor, "I knowed who this feller was the danged minute he rode in here. He's trouble and gunplay and a pine box, you ask me. I seed his kind afore, up in the Gulch, in Ginny City, and a hundred places in between. His hands are as smooth as tanned cow leather and he never sits with his back to the door and always sleeps with one eye open. Oh, I reckon I know who this feller is. I seen 'em plant many sech in boot hill graveyards from Laramie to Bannock."

"Well, listen, Jake," said Proctor. "He was a pard of Ned Grover's and he come here to help."

"Shit," said Wheeler. "This town's a keg of dynamite as it is and it looks like this feller's just the kind who'll put a torch to it. Say one thing for him, though. He takes care of his horse. That Blaze is a fine piece of horseflesh."

Slocum didn't thank the man. Instead, he got his tack and began saddling his horse. Men like Jake Wheeler were the salt of the earth. In his time he had probably seen a lot of trouble, and he was wise to trust only the animals under his care. He had learned one thing, though: Herb Unger was undoubtedly the man who had shot at him that morning. Unger was the man who had been hunting Ebenezer Lee, and from the looks of things, Lee was still alive.

Proctor finished saddling up a claybank mare and the two men rode out the back of the stables. Slocum said nothing as they rode to the edge of the town, where Proctor halted on a little knoll that overlooked the back of the stables, the corrals behind it.

"We'll just set a spell," he said, "see if anyone rides out after us."

"You said something back there," said Slocum. "I guess you didn't want Wheeler to know what it was."

"Oh, I trust Jake," said Dewey, "but I'm not sayin' someone bad couldn't beat it out of him. Me 'n' Eb had a agreement that if somethin' happened, I was to ride to a partic'lar place at night and light up a pine torch. He said he'd come down if he was still alive. And, if he didn't, he was likely dead."

"Where is this place?" asked Slocum.

"Up yonder," said Proctor. "Near the high meadow. We got us a meetin' spot. If Eb's alive, he'll be where he can see that pitchpine burnin'. You game to ride? It'll be colder'n hell, time we get up there."

"Yes," said Slocum.

"Uh-oh," said Proctor, and Slocum looked down the slope. The stable doors opened at the back and golden light spilled into the corral. Shadows of mounted men passed in front of the light.

"I count four. No, five," said Proctor in a harsh whisper.

"Five," Slocum agreed.

"Take us a little longer to get where we're a-goin'. That damned Injun's with 'em."

"That looked like Unger in the lead."

"It was."

"Who's the Indian?" asked Slocum.

"Oh, you ain't met him yet. Blackfoot name of Red Sky. He can track a man over rock. Carberry uses him, time to time. A trading post Injun. Give him enough whiskey and he'll cut his own brother's heart out and eat it for breakfast."

"Maybe we shouldn't ride up there just yet," said Slocum.

"Naw, we got to see if Eb needs help. I was a-goin' up there anyways. Still can, you want to back out."

Proctor was testing him, Slocum knew.

"No, I'll go with you, Proctor. We've got twenty, thirty minutes on them now."

"I reckon we'll have to give 'em a ride, do some doublin' back. Two of those men follered me to the hotel after I left you. They're hard and they ain't strangers to sleepin' out on cold nights."

Slocum knew, then, what he was facing. These were hard men following them. Evidently, they had planned this all along. He had the feeling that he had never been much out of sight of at least one of Carberry's men the whole time he'd been in town. The thought gave him an eerie feeling.

He wondered if Proctor knew what he was doing. The odds had swung wildly all of a sudden.

It was five to two in Carberry's favor.

9

Dewey Proctor picked the trail. Slocum followed, giving Blaze his head. The miner criss-crossed the slope, his horse stepping over live springs, downed timber, following a course the animal apparently knew well. At times the two animals floundered through deep snowdrifts, and once, Slocum heard one of their pursuers curse. The sound carried far on the night air, gave the illusion that the men following Slocum and the miner were much closer than they actually were. It was cold, and Slocum was glad he had new gloves and socks. He was warm inside the sheepskin jacket, and his hands and feet would not succumb to the chill.

"I packed plenty of grub, case we have to stay a few days," Proctor said, when they stopped to rest. The going got rougher the higher they climbed. Proctor patted his bulging saddlebags.

"How about Eb?"

"He may need some grub, too," said Proctor laconically.

Slocum wondered if Eb Lee was still alive. From the tracks he had seen that morning, the man could be wounded. He was afoot, no doubt, and if he couldn't stop bleeding or stay warm, he might not survive the bitter cold of this night. The temperature, Slocum figured, must be well below the freezing point.

The two men rode silently, paralleling the slope for a

ways, then Proctor switched back again. His horse had to struggle up the grade, muscles bunched, to gain headway through the drifts. When the moon rose, the forest took on an eerie appearance. Deep shadows lunged into bone-white patches in the open where the snow glittered like thick will-o'-the-wisp, like the fox-fire mists he had seen in Missouri and Arkansas during the War.

At the higher elevation, the snow was crusted from wind and freezing temperatures. Proctor let his mount pick its way. The crust could cut a horse's delicate ankles, could cripple an animal. Slocum followed patiently, listening hard for pursuers, hearing only the crunch of snow, the labored breathing of the horses. He had long since lost all sense of direction. The moon bleached the land, painted it in a surreal glow, made the night seem even colder than it was.

Finally, Proctor topped the ridge, and Slocum located the Big Dipper, the North Star, and got his bearings. Proctor rode along the ridge for a time, heading north, then swung east, toward the long valley below. As far as Slocum could determine, they were not following any regular trail, only going by Proctor's knowledge of the land, or maybe by his instincts.

Their breaths blew frosty plumes in the moonlight as they wound their way through pines and junipers, fir and spruce trees. Soon Slocum saw the valley through the trees, saw the wide band of white gleaming in the spooky light of the moon. Still, Proctor rode on, skirting the edge of the valley, staying on the slope. He stopped once and did not speak. Slocum listened to the soundless night and heard nothing. Not a sound.

Proctor shrugged and Slocum caught a glimpse of his face before he turned and dug boot heels into his horse's flanks. The man's face was gaunt and colorless in the moonlight, the eyes hollow as the sockets in a skull. Only the smoke of his breath gave life to that death's head visage. Slocum shuddered, feeling now the cold seeping through his coat.

Finally, Dewey Proctor reined up and waited for Slocum. The man looked around in the darkness, cupped a hand to his ear.

"We'll hide the horses near that deadfall over there," said Proctor, pointing to a dark shadow made by the tangled branches of a fallen tree. Slocum nodded and dismounted. Proctor did the same. They tied the horses several feet apart, kept the ropes high so they wouldn't become entangled. Proctor unwrapped the bundle with the pine knot kindling and handed half of the sticks to Slocum.

"Bring your rifle. May need it."

"How about yours?"

"One'll be enough, likely."

Slocum shrugged, jerked his rifle free of its scabbard. He put the chunks of wood in the pockets of his jacket, leaving his hands free.

"Come on," said the miner. "We've got some walkin' to do."

"Lead out," said Slocum.

Proctor's mention of "some walkin' to do" was an understatement. The two men clambered over deadfalls, struggled through hip-high drifts, slipped from tree to tree. Proctor back-trailed, jumped, doubled back, and led them in circles, but Slocum realized that the man knew what he was doing. All the time they kept moving toward some predetermined destination, but the miner was laying down a confusing set of tracks. There were times when he would stop and brush out their tracks, using a pine limb to smooth out the snow where it had not crusted.

Proctor was good, Slocum admitted. But he didn't know if such a trail could slow a good tracker. If that Blackfoot, Red Sky, was any good at all, he would not be fooled.

Eventually, their seemingly aimless meandering led the two men to a slash in the timber, a long downslope that had been cut by an ancient landslide. Here Proctor halted at the edge of the timber, scanned the empty expanse for a long time before he spoke.

"This is the cut where Eb'll be watching," Dewey whispered. "We'll set out three pitchpine stobs, three feet apart in a line, and light 'em up."

"Then what?" asked Slocum.

"Then we hide out here in the timber and wait."

"Lee will come to us?"

"If'n he's alive," said Proctor.

And, Slocum thought, *if someone else doesn't get to us first*.

They set out the pitchpine faggots. Proctor struck a sulphur match, set them afire. Then the two men floundered back into the timber. They waited, watching the torches burn, paint the snow with orange flame.

"What happens when they burn out?" Slocum asked. Although they had swept the snow away and rammed the stakes into the frozen earth, one of the torches was leaning precariously.

"We light three more. We keep it up all night, if need be, or until we run out of pitchpine."

They watched the pine burn, watched until the fires sputtered and went out. Then they went out into the open again and repeated the procedure. In the silence, they listened to the crackle of the burning pine, listened for the sound of a footfall. The air seemed colder now, and they could feel the beginnings of a night wind on their faces.

Slocum assessed their chances, silently and to himself. If Ebenezer Lee could see the burning torches, it might take him a long time to climb the steep slope. He could be above or below them, or across the valley. That latter was the most likely. And, by any measurement, that was a long walk through deep snow. As the minutes dragged on, Slocum began to worry about the men who had followed them out of town. If they came to this open slash, they'd see the torches, too, and then all the hardcases would have to do would be to wait. It was a hellish situation, any way you looked at it.

The longer they waited, the more Slocum didn't like it. Proctor was restless as well. He kept tromping his feet to keep them warm, and his coat brushed up against the bark of a pine, making Slocum jump. Noise. It traveled far on the wind and a good tracker could make sense of it. The sound of tree branches rubbing was different from the sound of antlers against wood, or a man's coat scratching at bark.

Again, the pitchpine torches burned out. Without saying anything to Slocum, Proctor stepped out into the open. The wood rattled in his hands. "You just as well wait here," said Dewey. "Don't take two of us to light these."

Slocum hefted his rifle, just in case. He waited in the shadows of the pines, watched the lone figure lean into the growing wind, head for the spot where the torches flickered their last.

They both heard it: the snap of a branch on the other side of the clear swath. Slocum went into a crouch, instinctively, brought the rifle to his shoulder. Dewey hesitated, looked across the empty frozen expanse.

"Get down!" yelled Slocum.

But his call was too late. A rifle cracked, and orange flame blossomed into a deadly flower from the timber a hundred yards off. Proctor twitched, pitched forward, headlong into the snow.

"Oh, Christ!" yelled Dewey.

Slocum jacked a cartridge into the chamber, fired at the lingering image of the orange blossom. He heard a grunt and a curse. Slocum fired again, then duck-waddled toward Proctor, staying low, levering another shell into the chamber of his rifle.

Another shot rang out, a crisp crack of exploded powder and snowdust kicked up near Dewey. Slocum saw the fire flash and swung his barrel, snapped off another shot. He crawled, then, toward Dewey, ignoring the cold, the slash of the crusted snow on his shins and forearms.

"Christ, Slocum, I got hit bad," said the miner as Slocum snaked toward him.

"Be quiet. I'm going to drag you to cover. Just lie quiet. Don't try to help."

Proctor groaned. Slocum hugged the snow as another shot boomed and the angry whine of a bullet creased the air overhead. The bullet hit the snow a few yards away, plowed a six-foot furrow. Slocum grabbed Dewey's collar, began to inch backward toward the timber.

Rifles cracked from three different directions, but the shots were wild. The darkness and the glow of the snow made sighting tricky, Slocum knew. He fired once, then shifted his position. He hunched over Proctor, put his arms under the miner's shoulders. Then he crawled on his knees toward the protection of the woods as the snow kicked up around him with the rip of lead bullets.

Proctor groaned, but Slocum could not tell how badly the man was hit. He hated moving him like this, but he had no choice. If they stayed out in the open, neither one of them would survive. Eventually those bullets would find their marks.

Slocum tugged, scrambled the last few yards. He pulled Proctor behind a tree, shoved fresh cartridges into his rifle's magazine. A man stepped out of the timber on the opposite side, and Slocum drew a bead on him, fired, adjusting for the tricky light, the darkness. He saw the man throw up his arms and drop his rifle. A split-second later, the man cried out and fell backward onto the hard crust of the snow.

Another rifle cracked and wood splintered off the pine six inches from Slocum's ear. He ducked, worked the lever of his rifle. Whatever happened, they couldn't stay here. Someone on the other side had the range now. Another shot and a ball ricocheted off the tree with an angry snarl.

"Slocum, Jesus, they got me," said Dewey.

John backed away from the tree as two more shots rang out. He heard the bullets buzz as they went by, the crackle as they broke tree branches several yards behind him. He leaned over the wounded man, touched his coat. He felt the stickiness of blood on his fingers.

Gunshot, he thought. Quickly, he unbuttoned Proctor's coat, lay it aside like flesh stripped from a deer. In the pale glow of light, he saw the dark stain spreading across Dewey's middle. He reached behind him, feeling for an exit wound. The ball was still in him, or else had come out somewhere else. Slocum had seen that happen. Once a lead ball got inside a man, rammed against bone and muscle, it could veer off at any angle. Same with critters. Either way, it was serious. If there was no exit wound, Proctor might not bleed to death as quickly. If the ball had cut through any arteries, it wouldn't make any difference. He'd die quick. If the ball stayed inside him, he'd die a slow, lingering, painful death. What Proctor needed was a doctor—or a preacher.

"Bad?" the miner asked as Slocum buttoned his coat back up.

"You're bleeding some."

"Feels like fire in my belly," gasped the wounded man.

"Stay quiet and we'll get you out of this."

"How bad is it, John? I didn't feel much when I got hit. Felt like somebody hit me with a sixteen-pound maul square in the belly."

"You shouldn't talk, Dewey," said Slocum, trying not to choke up.

"Damn it, man, stay on the level with me."

"You'll make it if you do what I say," said Slocum, suddenly angry. He was angry at the man who had shot Proctor, at himself, at death.

"I'll do 'er," said Proctor, gritting his teeth. Slocum felt the man's body shudder with pain. "Whatever you say, John Slocum."

Slocum started to say something, but he held his silence. He had lied to the man enough. Already, the smell of death seemed to rise up from Proctor like steam.

He knew if they didn't move from this place, they would both die. Already he could hear the men moving around across the slash.

Soon, he knew, they would be coming for him. And even if he had killed one man, maybe wounded another, he was still outnumbered three to one.

Slocum knew what he had to do. He just hoped he had time and strength to do it.

His chances, he knew, were slim to none. And none was looking pretty big right then.

10

Slocum knew he would have to get to the horses eventually, but first he had to find a defendable shelter for him and Proctor. To do that, he would have to move the wounded man. Or would he? Moving a gutshot man was dangerous. He suspected that Dewey was bleeding internally. If he was kept still, Proctor had a chance to live. The blood could coagulate if the bleeding was confined to veins. Right now, Slocum didn't think any arteries had been damaged. The blood flow was not strong enough. The wound in Proctor's belly was seeping blood, not gushing it.

"Dewey, you lie still. I'm going to dig us a hole."

"Huh?"

"Just sit tight. I'll be back."

Slocum crawled away, found a large tree that had fallen. Its bulk had kept the snow from accumulating on one side, and that was where he began to set up a temporary shelter. There was enough brush around the tree to hide them if he dug a shallow hole. He could defend the position, too, if necessary. Slocum figured on a long night.

Using his knife, Slocum cut dead boughs, stacked them against the fallen tree. He made a bed of pine needles and balsam, working quickly, listening to every sound. When he was satisfied, he went back to where he had left Proctor.

"Slocum, that you?"

"Yeah. I have to move you, Dewey."

"Christ, it hurts."

"Hang on." Slocum retrieved one of the pitchpine sticks from his pocket, put the small, pointed end into Proctor's mouth. "Bite down on this," he said. Gingerly, he picked the miner up, slung him over his shoulders. Quickly, he dashed back to the fallen tree.

He lay Proctor in the shelter. The man's face was drenched with sweat. Fresh blood seeped through Dewey's jacket. The miner spit out the stick of wood, gasped for breath.

"Damn, Slocum, I think you tore something loose."

"Just lie flat and I'll cold-pack your wound with snow. Might help stop the blood."

"There ain't much more pain I can stand," said the miner.

"I know," Slocum said.

He made the man comfortable, leaned his rifle against the log to keep it handy. He unbuttoned Dewey's coat, pulled up his woolen shirt and flannel undershirt. Fresh blood poured from the bullet hole, but it wasn't a rush as he had expected. Quickly, Slocum began to pack the wound with snow. Proctor winced, bit his lip to keep from crying out in pain. Slocum put freezing snow on Proctor's belly, tamped it down, then pulled his clothes back together.

"Some whiskey'd do me good," muttered Proctor.

"No. Even if I had any..."

"Water, then."

"Wouldn't be good. Wait'll I get that bleeding stopped, Dewey."

"Christ."

Slocum knew it would be bad. He hunkered down

behind the deadfall, listened intently. He heard a branch snap and felt his palms go clammy. A horse, from far across the slash, whickered. *Maybe,* he thought, *they'll wait for daybreak before they move in.* But he didn't believe that entirely.

As if in reply to his thoughts, a rifle cracked nearby, and he heard the zing-whine of a bullet probe the darkness overhead. He saw no muzzle flash, but he marked the spot, and peered over the top of the log. A few seconds later, another shot boomed, and this time he saw the orange ball of fire, the quick puff of white smoke that disappeared in the darkness. The bullet slashed branches off as it passed several yards from him.

Slocum did not return fire. From the two shots, he knew that the rifleman wasn't sure. He had the general direction down pat, but not Slocum's exact location.

It grew quiet, then, and the stillness was agonizing. Proctor moaned softly, and Slocum felt a twinge in his gut. The miner was tough, but his belly must be hurting him bad.

The silence stretched and the wind rose, bringing the temperature down. Slocum heard nothing for a long time. Finally, he saw a distant flash of orange through the trees.

The arrogant bastards, he thought. It was obvious and unnerving that Unger's bunch were so sure of themselves that they had made camp for the night. That meant that someone was probably guarding his and Proctor's horses, waiting in ambush, just waiting for one or both of them to return. Slocum cursed silently. He was shivering in the cold, Proctor was dying, and Unger's bunch had a blazing fire going. *The sons of bitches.*

Proctor groaned low in his throat, and Slocum bent over him, listened to his thready breathing. He wondered if Dewey was still bleeding. He wasn't going to check now. As long as the miner was breathing, there was hope.

"Slocum," the wounded man rasped.

"Yeah?"

"Maybe we better get on out of here. I feel real bad."

"They've got us pinned down, Dewey. Right now, we've got some shelter, and they aren't exactly sure where we are. If we get caught out in the open tonight, that wind will freeze us to rock."

"That's how your friend Grover died. He was found frozen. Might have saved him, if he'd—"

"You saying that Ned didn't die right away?"

"Nope. He was shot, left out to die. His horse come in, but not Ned. Fact is, someone brung his horse in. Grover had been left to die slow."

Slocum swore.

What kind of men were these, he wondered, who shot a man, then left him to freeze to death? Such acts went beyond greed. Carberry must enjoy killing. Maybe the taking of another man's life gave him a sense of power, of omnipotence. Slocum had known such men, their sensibilities twisted like wind-blown cedars growing out of rimrock. Men with warped souls, cloudy little dark minds.

Dewey reached out and grabbed Slocum's wrist. He squeezed it hard. "Damn, I'm hurting real bad, Slocum."

"Yeah, Dewey, I know. Are you cold?"

"Some, but it ain't bad. Mostly, I feel that fire in my gut and it goes up my backbone straight to my brain."

"You'll have to grit it out," said Slocum.

They were still out there, he knew, Unger and his bunch. They were like winter wolves on the prowl, hungry, searching, sniffing. Well, one of them was hurting, too—or dead. That was little consolation now, but it was better than nothing. He had hurt them some, anyway. They would respect his rifle, if not him. That was probably why they didn't come after him and Dewey in the dark.

Slocum moved away from Dewey. He picked up a chunk of wood and threw it off into the brush.

A rifle cracked from less than a hundred yards away.

Yes, Slocum thought, *they're still out there, and they know where we are*.

Herb Unger hunkered by the fire, but he didn't look directly into its blaze. He heard the rifle crack once again and looked into the faces of the other men. Red Sky's visage was like a slab of leather, impassive as stone. The Blackfoot squatted there, his blanket wrapped around him, his rifle across his lap. Stan Loomis sat next to Dalbert Fricke, his withered left hand wrapped in a pair of socks, eyes glittering. Fricke, the dumb son of a bitch, was dying. He lay stretched out on the ground, staring into the fire with glazed eyes, blood seeping out of the corners of his mouth.

Frank Gliddens, the big bull, was keeping Slocum and Proctor pinned down. Unger would relieve him in an hour, and then it was Red Sky's turn.

"Mebbeso this Slocum he fly like grouse," said Red Sky, breaking the silence.

"He won't," said Unger.

"Better kill quick."

'Can you see in the dark, Injun?"

"Can hear."

"Hell, you want to sneak up on that bastard, go ahead," said Unger. "He's already put Dal down and he damned near put Stan's lights out."

"Him shoot good," admitted the Blackfoot. "Better kill now, no track when sun comes."

"He ain't goin' far, Sky. We damned sure shot Proctor. There's blood all over the snow out there. Slocum won't leave him."

"Mebbeso, you find horses belong Slocum. Kill horses, him no ride from mountain."

"You got a point there, Sky," said Unger. "Stan?"

"Yeah. I blazed in here. I can find 'em again." Loomis waved his withered hand, flopping the socks that covered it. "Red Sky may be right. If Slocum gets to a horse, he could cover some ground."

"Shit," said Unger. "We're about two, three men short. Damn Carberry, anyway."

"Hell, five against two wasn't bad," said Loomis.

"Damned Dalbert anyway. He should of been more careful," said Unger.

Dalbert Fricke moaned. He had a bullet in his lung, and now the blood was frothing up with bubbles. He made a gurgling sound in his throat. Loomis looked down at the dying man, shook his head. He took out a bag of Durham, grabbed the string in his teeth. Then he rolled a quirly, using his one good hand and the withered one for balance. He lighted the cigarette by bending down close to the fire. The smell of hair burning hung acrid in the air.

Unger kicked at the snow under his feet, growled low in his throat.

"I should have killed that son of a bitch when I had him cold," he muttered.

"Who?" asked Loomis.

Unger stood up, looked into the darkness.

"Slocum," he said, and walked away from the fire.

There was no way to shut Proctor up without killing him. The wounded miner was babbling now. When Slocum touched a hand to his cheek, he felt the fever in the man. Dewey was burning up. At first John hadn't been able to understand what Proctor was saying, but now he heard his name mentioned.

"Slocum, Slocum, you got to listen to me, man."

"What is it, Dewey?" Slocum bent over, spoke in a whisper. At the same time, he knew he had to listen for sounds. The Indian, or one of the others, could sneak up on them at any time. They had to know that Proctor was hurt bad and that they both couldn't sleep at the same time. Unger had enough men to crowd him in shifts, Slocum knew, and his nerves were already frazzled from Proctor's delirious babble, the knowledge that they were pinned down by at least one gun.

"I ain't got much time. Maybe you could get back in town, talk to her."

"Who?"

"You know. The woman."

"The only woman I met down there was Amy Nichols. Works in the general store."

"That's her. She was Ned's gal."

"Ned Grover's girl? You sure about that?"

"Sure as I'm dyin', Slocum. She may know who killed your pard."

"Damn," said Slocum. Ned had never mentioned her, but he could see now why she wanted to talk to him. Ned had probably told her all about his friend Slocum.

"You got to get out of here, son," said Proctor, lucid once again.

"We'll get out," Slocum said tightly.

"No, just you. I know Unger—he's got us pinned down tight as a butterfly on a board."

"If we get caught out in the open, with the wind like it is, we'll freeze," said Slocum.

"That was how it was with your friend Grover. They found him, shot, but froze to death. Damn, Slocum, I'm—I'm hurtin' real bad again. You got to go. Now."

"I'll stay with you, Dewey."

As if to emphasize his decision, the rifle cracked again, and a probing bullet thunked into the deadfall. *So, they know where we are,* thought Slocum. He couldn't leave now if he wanted to. Dewey wouldn't last ten minutes. Whoever was out there would finish him off.

"I heard 'im," said Dewey, his voice a throaty whisper. He coughed, then cried out in pain. Slocum held him down until the spasm passed.

"Listen, Slocum," Proctor husked, "and listen good. You got to go afore daylight. You go to the ridge on the other side of the valley. Look for a deep cut, a ravine wide enough for a herd of buffalo. You ride up there, look for the big arrowhead on a flat rock. Looks just like a arrowhead. Worn there by wind 'n' rain. You hear me?"

"I hear you. Keep talking, Dewey."

"That there arrowhead points straight down to where Eb's done blasted through to the biggest vein of silver you ever seed. Thick old cedars in there, and some spruce, so it's read hard to find."

"I'll find it if I can," said Slocum.

"Listen. Eb, he hauled all the tailings to another spot, so it's real hard to find. Pretty smart, eh? They's a cave big enough to crawl into, and Eb's got grub and stuff in there. Man could hold off a whole damned army. . . ."

Proctor's voice trailed away and his body shook with convulsions. Slocum grabbed him by the shoulders, felt the strength in the man. Then, suddenly, Proctor's body went limp. Slocum touched a finger to a place behind the miner's ear, felt for a pulse.

The feverish skin was already beginning to cool. There was no sign of life.

Dewey Proctor was dead.

11

Slocum stretched out Proctor's body and covered him with dead boughs. He did not say any words over the dead man. His first priority was to get back to the horse and shake his pursuers. As long as he was up here, they would dog his trail, keep him from finding Eb Lee. Eb, if he was alive, would be holed up at the mine, most likely, and one more night wouldn't make much difference. Besides, Slocum doubted he could find the ravine Proctor had spoken of—not in the dark, anyway. His best bet was to head back to town, leave before dawn when he could see by daylight.

He began to crawl away from the deadfall. A rifle shot crashed the stillness. The ball thunked into the trunk of a tree not three feet from Slocum's position. The shooter had changed position, was no longer on the other side of the log. Slocum saw the flash, realized he was exposed. The bushwacker had outflanked him!

Quickly, he brought his rifle up, got to his knees. He waddled to a tree for cover. A rifle shot greeted his move, and snow kicked up a foot from his face. He saw the orange explosion, fired instinctively. He heard no sound that his bullet had found the mark. "Damn," he muttered.

Well, one man, that was all. The shooter was probably circling him, moving. Just one, though. Which one? The Blackfoot? Unger? One of the others, perhaps. He was pretty good. If his only task was to keep Slocum pinned down, he was doing damned good.

Slocum stood up, using the tree for cover. As long as he let the shooter have the upper hand, he would be helpless. He had to break out, either kill the man or elude him. But how?

There was a way, if he could find it. Slocum looked at the trees, tried to fix on several that stood in a line. He would be taking a chance, but he had to try it. To stay where he was meant freezing to death or eventually getting shot. Neither alternative was acceptable.

Even in the dim moonlight, he could make out the shapes and comparative sizes of the trees. He picked a line that would take him on an angle toward the last position of the shooter. He levered another shell into the chamber, then ducked. He ran toward the nearest tree as fast as his feet would carry him through the snow. The rifle boomed. Slocum saw the fireflash off to his left, a few yards from where the gunman had fired from before. As soon as he hit the tree, he slid around to the right side, then raced toward the next tree in line. The ambusher did not shoot. Slocum did not wait, but ran to the next tree. This time the outlaw fired.

Slocum was still to the right of the shooter. He raced to the next tree. Then he slid around to the left and waited. He listened. He heard the brush crackle as a heavy body moved through it at a goodly clip.

"My turn," said Slocum, firing at the noise. He heard the bullet rip through brush, tear bark off a tree. Then he heard a man say something that sounded like "shit!" Slocum smiled.

He had the man worried now. Quickly, Slocum jacked the empty hull out and heard another bullet slide up in its place, filling the chamber. He ran to the next tree. No one shot at him.

He kept going, from tree to tree, drawing fire, but gradually circling, getting closer to his man. He made plenty of noise to keep the bushwhacker's interest. It had become a game. A deadly game of cat and mouse, or cat and cat.

Another shot sounded. Slocum saw the orange sparks as he peered from behind a tree. The man was no more than twenty yards away, Slocum figured. The trick now was to get the shooter to expose himself. Slocum set his rifle against the tree. He drew his .44 Remington, cocked it quietly by holding the trigger in slightly as he hammered back. The locking sear made no sound. Slocum waited, letting the silence grow like a cloud.

He watched, straining his eyes against the dark, not moving his head. Finally, he saw a human shape detach itself from the trunk of a tree not more than a dozen yards away. From the looks of him, the man was huge. It wasn't the Indian. It wasn't Unger. Slocum knew that much. He saw the man's rifle held at an angle across his chest, the barrel pewtered by the moonlight.

One step more, Slocum thought, as the big man hesitated.

The silence stretched like a tautened leather thong. Still, Frank Gliddens hesitated. He seemed poised on the brink of eternity for one agonizing moment. Then he stepped into the open and Slocum got a glimpse of his full size.

"Looking for me?" Slocum said, as he took deadly aim on the man's chest.

Gliddens started to raise his rifle. Slocum squeezed the trigger, saw the man's bulky form disappear in a flash of powder, a cloud of white smoke. Then he heard a gasp, followed by a resounding thump as the giant crashed to the ground. Slocum ran toward him, zigzagging. He reached the man in less than a dozen strides.

Gliddens lay face down in the snow. He was not breathing. There was a big hole in his shoulder that glistened in the moonlight. Slocum touched the wound, but the blood was no longer pumping through. He hunkered down, felt the man's pulse at his neck. There was none.

Slocum strode back to the tree and retrieved his rifle. He wasted no more time, but began to lope through the forest, looking up at the Big Dipper to keep his bearings. He put distance between him and the dead man, followed the natural slope down to the place where he and Proctor had left the horses tied. He stopped every so often to listen, but he heard no sound of anyone on his trail.

When he drew close to the deadfall where they had tied their mounts, Slocum slowed down. He circled, closing in on the spot cautiously. The outlaws might have left a guard behind, or they might send someone at any moment to cut him off.

He heard Blaze whicker. Then Proctor's horse neighed.

Slocum kept low, moved in an erratic pattern toward the horses. Finally, he crept on them. They had not been disturbed, but there were other tracks there. Horses had passed by, close enough to see Blaze and the other animal. With no time to waste, Slocum untied the horses and mounted Blaze.

He moved through the woods like a ghost, angling back toward the trail that would lead him to Silverado. He kept a steady pace and when he found the trail he breathed out in relief. Soon he saw the lights of the town below and he raked spurs gently against Blaze's flanks. He looked up at the night sky and judged the hour to be near midnight.

Midnight. It was, he thought, an unseemly hour to be calling on a woman he had just met. But then, he did not know Amy Nichols very well.

She was waiting for him, not inside the boarding house, as he had expected, but on the porch, wrapped in a heavy coat, pacing back and forth, her breath visible on the cold night air. Slocum had left Proctor's horse in the stables, ridden straight for Mrs. Willoughby's boarding house. A white sign out front proclaimed the dwelling as such. Slocum dismounted outside the white picket fence, wrapped the reins around the hitchrail.

"John Slocum," she whispered loudly, "is that you, finally?"

"Yes'm," he said.

"Oh, thank goodness. I was afraid something had happened to you. Are you all right?"

"Yes, ma'am. I'm fine."

She rushed down the porch to the gate and opened it for him.

"Come inside," she said. "You look frozen. I've a fire and whiskey if you like."

He was surprised at her friendliness, at the urgency of her tone. He wondered if Mrs. Willoughby allowed her female boarders to come and go at odd hours. He followed Amy up the walk. At the bottom of the steps, she hesitated.

"Don't worry about making any noise," she said. "I'm the only boarder here and Mrs. Willoughby, bless her heart, is sound asleep and stone deaf."

Handy, Slocum thought, but he said nothing. At least

that explained why Amy Nichols was standing out on the porch at midnight. The frame house was two-storied. The floors creaked when he entered, followed Amy past the parlor and down a short hall.

The room was large and cozy. A pair of lamps cast a coppery glow on doilied tables. There was a divan, an overstuffed chair, a hassock in front of it, and several straight-backed chairs. The fireplace crackled with light and heat. The room was warm, perfect for a winter evening.

"Take off your coat. Sit on the divan if you like."

Slocum took off his gloves and slipped out of his coat. Amy set the coat and gloves on a straight-backed chair, waved him to the divan. "Make yourself to home," she said, "while I get you a drink. Whiskey? I also have wine. I can mull it if you like, put a stick of cinnamon in it."

"Whiskey will do," he said. She smiled and he saw the genuine warmth of the smile, admired the white even teeth, the fullness of her lips. She went to a cabinet, opened it, and took out a bottle of whiskey. Atop the cabinet were some glasses. She took one, poured it to within a quarter inch of the rim.

"I'll have some mulled wine, I think," she said. "I took chill outside waiting for you."

"I'm sorry," said Slocum.

"It's not your fault," she said. "I was anxious. I've much to tell you, some things to talk about. Please, make yourself comfortable. I'll be right back."

He watched her go, marveling at her fluid grace, the curve of her hips, the trimness of her ankles. She was a beauty, with her soft dark hair and eyes, patrician features. He could see why Ned Grover would be attracted to her, why any man would.

Slocum sipped at his whiskey. The taste was familiar. Ned had never been one to like tanglefoot or Pop Skull. Old Overholt. That's what this was, and Slocum enjoyed its smooth bite, the warmth that spread through his belly.

He watched the flames dancing in the fireplace, thought of his friend who had died too young. Ned was a year or two younger than Slocum, cut from the same rough cloth. He had fought bravely in the War, had come through some close shaves. He was from Kentucky or Tennessee. Slocum never could get it straight. He had lived in both states, fought for the South. Ned was always for the underdog.

Amy appeared a few moments later, holding a large mug of steaming apple wine. She sat down next to Slocum and looked him over carefully. "I hope you weren't offended by your treatment at the store today. My boss is afraid of strangers. Carberry's bunch runs all over him. He didn't mean it personally. He's just a man who wants to please both sides and so ends up pleasing neither."

Slocum laughed. Amy Nichols was not only beautiful, she was smart, too. "I didn't pay much attention to it," he said, his green eyes flickering in the firelight like cut jade. "I've seen towns go bad before. Fear is like a plague. It spreads from man to man until everyone is jumpy, ready to shoot at the slightest noise."

"That's how Silverado has become," she admitted, daintily sipping her warm wine. "John—may I call you that?—Ned Grover was your friend. He and I were friends, and I had hoped one day to marry him. I didn't know him long, but he seemed a good man."

"That he was."

"He talked about you a great deal. I think he trusted

you more than any other man he knew."

"I trusted him, too, ma'am."

"Please, call me Amy. I know he was hoping you would come before—before . . ."

She started to break down then, but he saw her square her shoulders, take a deep breath, and blink back the tears.

"You had a big place in your heart for Ned," he said.

"Yes, John. A big place. I—I saw him killed. Murdered."

Slocum leaned forward, watching her intently. "Who killed him?"

"Herb Unger and Lucius Carberry."

"Just those two?"

"Yes. Eb Lee saw it too. It was horrible."

Slocum sucked in a breath.

"Lee saw him die?"

"Yes. I think that's one reason why Carberry's hunting Ebenezer. Lucius saw Eb, but not me."

"Are you sure?" asked Slocum.

"Pretty sure."

"What happened?"

"It was a mix-up. Ned left early that morning to take supplies up to Eb. But Eb rode by here and asked for Ned. I told him what happened, that Ned got a message to bring a mule up to the high valley that morning. The message was from Eb, supposedly, but it wasn't. Eb was furious and I was frantic."

"So?"

"Eb didn't want me to go along, but I knew something terrible was going to happen to Ned. I knew it in my heart. I insisted on going with Eb. We rode up the trail. I think when Ned didn't see Ebenezer at their regular meeting place, he knew something was wrong. He started to backtrack, and that's when Carberry and Unger caught him out in the open. They shot Ned several times. Eb made me stay hidden in the trees, but he rode out after them. Herb put Ned on his horse and the two men rode away. They shot at Eb Lee. He had to back away and it was getting dark. He came back to see that I was safe. We knew Ned was hurt badly and we wanted to follow them. We had no supplies, and it began to snow. We rode back into town. I was just sick. The next day, Eb rode back up the mountain and he found Ned lying on the rocks, frozen to death. He had been shot, but...oh, John, it must have been horrible for him!"

She began to sob then, and Slocum took her in his arms, tried to comfort her. It was as if she had held back her emotions for a long time and now they had been released. He felt her body shake as the sobs wracked her body.

"Cry it on out," he said soothingly.

"Damn, damn, damn," she wailed.

He rubbed her hair, trying to calm her down. She nestled close to him, her breasts pressing against his chest. She was soft and trembling in his arms and he knew there was nothing he would say that would take away the grief and the heartache of this young woman.

She had lost her husband-to-be, and he had lost a friend. It was no comfort to know that Carberry and Unger were still alive. Worse, they had killed another man, and Slocum didn't have the heart to tell Amy that Dewey Proctor was also dead.

"John," she said finally, drying her eyes, "I'm so glad you were here. I kept it all inside me. I—I felt so lost and helpless. But you, you were Ned's friend, and it's as if I've known you all my life. Hold me, hold me tight. I've needed someone strong to hold me like this."

"I understand," he said. "I'll stay as long as you need me. But I've got to go back up on the mountain tomorrow and find Ebenezer Lee. I think he's in danger."

"I heard you and Dewey rode up there. There was talk all over town. And Herb Unger—he went up there, too."

Slocum drew a breath, looked away from her.

"Where's Dewey?" she asked suddenly, her voice quavering on the verge of hysteria. "Did he come back with you?"

"Dewey won't be coming back, Amy. I'm sorry."

"Oh, no!" she cried, and he saw the terror in her eyes, the anger at forces she couldn't control. She grabbed him then, and burrowed her face in his chest. She held onto him tightly until he could feel her fingernails digging into his flesh.

"God, John," she sobbed, "don't leave me. Don't leave me now."

And he knew he would not leave her this night, not for any earthly reason.

12

Slocum didn't want to take advantage of Amy Nichols. He knew what grief could do to a woman. He had seen prim and proper women lose all sense of propriety in the grip of grief. He had seen normally chaste and reserved women lose all control when faced abruptly with the evidence of mortality. He thought maybe it had something to do with animal instinct, a desire to continue the species during times of famine, war, disaster.

He had seen women make love to strangers at the height of intense battle, oblivious to death or danger. He had seen widows take the first man to bed within hours or days after losing their husbands. It was as if they needed some assurance that they were still alive, that they were still desirable.

Still, Amy Nichols surprised him.

"John," she said softly, "would you think me wicked or shameless if I asked you to stay with me tonight?"

He knew what she meant, but he wasn't going to ruin her dignity. "Sure. I could bunk on the floor."

She took his hand in hers. "No, I didn't mean that. I want you to share my bed."

"Amy, you make it hard on a man."

"I don't think I could bear to be alone. Not tonight. Not when you're facing so much tomorrow."

"It wouldn't bother you?"

"No," she said. "I thought it would. I thought about

you a lot today. I wondered if you would actually come here and if we would talk. Then, when I saw you ride up, and when you put your arms around me . . . I just melted inside. I felt warm and safe for the first time since Ned . . . since Ned died. It's been just terrible."

She squeezed his hand in hers, looked at him with soft, limpid eyes. He could almost feel her squeezing his heart. There was no mistaking the anxious look in her eyes. Here was a woman in her youthful prime, and here was a woman in anguish. To turn her down would not only break her heart, it would crush her spirit. He couldn't do that to her, nor to himself. If he did not taste her sweets, he knew he would always regret it.

"You don't have to say any more," he said. "I understand. You're a beautiful young lady. A woman. I just wouldn't want to tread on territory where I wasn't welcome."

"Take advantage of me? Oh no, John Slocum. It wouldn't be that. I want you as I've never wanted a man before. Even . . . well, let's just say you stir things in me that no other man has before. Maybe it's Fate, or whatever you want to call it, but I feel you came to Silverado for a reason. What happened before was meant to be. Do you ever feel that way?"

"Sometimes," he lied.

She scooted close to him, put her arms around his neck, and drew his mouth to hers. They kissed and the kiss was warm and sweet. He slid his tongue inside her mouth, felt her response. Her breasts rubbed against his chest and he felt her body begin to writhe as he clasped her in a vigorous embrace.

"Oh, John," she breathed. "I want you so much."

"Yes," he husked, and he felt his loins churn with

desire, felt the heat surge through his manhood like fiery lava.

"Take me," she said. "Take me to bed." •

He had no hunger but the hunger for her. He watched her turn down the lamps, forgot about his unfinished drink. She came to him in the darkness, slipped her arm around his waist, led him down the hall to her bed-chamber. There, a single lamp glowed low, and the bed was in shadow, the coverlet turned back, the pillows fluffed full.

"Hurry," she whispered, and her voice purred with promise. He began to undress, watching her as she slipped out of her frock, daintily removed her under-things. When they were both naked, they stood there for a moment, looking at each other, the lust in their eyes throwing off sparks. She glided to the bed, sat on its edge, regarding him.

"Yes," she said, "I want you. You—you're a hand-some man, a loving man."

Her breasts were full and uptilted. He wondered briefly if Ned had ever tasted her honey. It was not a question he would ask, but it crossed his mind. If he had, then she was the better for it, but if he hadn't, it was no wonder that Amy needed a man. She must have felt cheated, deprived, when Ned died. It could happen to a woman. To a man as well.

"Do you still want me?" he asked, feeling like an idiot.

"As I've never wanted anyone before, John." She held out her arms to him, beckoned him with a half-smile, an alluring toss of her head. Her body turned tawny in the lampglow and his gaze roamed over her flawless flesh. The hunger built in him, too, and as he strode to her, his manhood hardened almost imperceptibly and the heat roiled his loins to the boiling point.

She grasped his manhood, stroked it lovingly as he stood there before her.

"Woman, you know just what to do," he husked.

"I want you inside me," she said huskily.

"Yeah," said Slocum. "It's time." She slinked across the bed, lay on her back, her legs slightly spread, her back arched, like a queen reclining on her royal pallet, arms open to receive him.

He blanketed her with his body, pried her legs farther apart with his knees, slipped between them. He kissed her on the mouth, kissed her breasts, felt her body arch as he slid his hands to the small of her back.

"Take me, take me," she moaned.

He rose above her, slid closer to her. She grasped his swollen staff and guided it to her sex. He slipped inside the portal, filled her. She bucked with a sudden orgasm and he felt her fingernails dig into his back as she grabbed him.

"Oh, yes," she sighed, "oh, yes, John."

He plumbed her depths, sliding in and out, his manhood brushing against the trigger of pleasure that made her undulate and writhe beneath his powerful body. She buckled under a wave of pleasure as an orgasmic quake shuddered through her and she screamed softly in his ear.

He burrowed into her, knew that she was no virgin, but a woman fullblown, as desirable as any he had ever known. She matched him in fervor and vigor, yet she was soft and pliant, kittenish and bold. Her loins quivered when he sank deep inside her, and when she brought her legs together, her muscles squeezed him with sensual pressure. He began to stroke her faster and she rocked with him, their loins slapping together in perfect rhythm. He drank in the heady scent of her musk, gazed down at her glistening breasts, smeared now with both their sweat, the dark nipples rising pertly out of bubbled aureoles that seemed perfectly symmetrical. His hands kneaded her buttocks, pulled her to him so that he drove still deeper, clear to the mouth of her womb.

Again and again, Amy thrashed with orgasmic explosions and held onto him tightly, her fingernails raking his back, drawing blood. But Slocum felt no pain, only the firecracker explosions in his brain that showered him with purest raw pleasure.

"Yes, yes," she screamed, urging him on, and Slocum felt the swirl of heat in his loins, the incredible rush. He tried to stay it, but there was no turning back. His mind flashed dark, then light, then dark again as he came with mighty spurts that drained away his strength, left him limp and helpless. He lay atop her, gasping for breath as she soothed him with love words and stroked his back with her gentle hands.

She let out a sigh of exhaustion and kissed his damp forehead before he rolled off her and lay beside her, a sated giant basking after a battle, his chest rising and falling with his every breath.

"It was wonderful," she whispered. "You were magnificent."

"Umm, yes, Amy," he said. "It was good. You were good."

"I never felt anything like that in my life," she said. "I'm giddy from it. I feel weak and yet oddly stimulated. All over."

"It's a good feeling."

She touched his sweat-soaked body, roamed his flesh with her fingers, exulting in the power she had unleashed and which now lay tame and conquered beside her. She looked at him with a starry-eyed gaze. It was a look of wonder and of triumph, of gratitude and of savage pride.

"I can still feel you inside me," she said.

He felt nothing now, only a lassitude, a calm that washed over him like a subsiding tide. But he felt good and when he looked into her eyes, he felt a tug of fear, for here was a woman who had lost all reason, who saw him as something other than he was. He was a man, not a god, yet the look in her eyes was one of awe and there was no mistaking the flush of pleasure that lingered like rosy light on her cheeks. She squeezed his deflated flesh as if hoping to make it rise again, and she smiled at him with a knowing look in her eyes.

"Give me about fifteen or twenty minutes," he laughed, and she squeezed him again.

He awoke with a start, wondered where he was. He felt the soft body next to him, her nakedness, and it came back to him. He had taken her twice more and then sleep had dragged them away, folded them under drugged blankets.

Amy. Even in the dark, he could sense her beauty, the unbridled lust in her loins, her breasts, the wise glint of her eyes. She was a woman, and then some, and he hated to leave her and go back up on that mountain where he faced cold and death. It was so warm here, so quiet and peaceful.

Slocum tried to get back to sleep, but he slept fitfully, and finally arose from the bed and dressed. He lit the lamps in the living room, checked his guns, and wiped them down. He sat on the divan for a long time after that, thinking over his strategy when he returned to the high valley. He also tried not to think of Jezebel all alone up there, wondering what had happened to her father.

Sometime later, he went outside and saddled Blaze, made sure that his canteens were full. He had plenty of ammunition, enough jerky, hardtack, and coffee to keep him alive for a few days. When he returned from the stables, he saw the glow of lamps in the kitchen window. The back door opened. Amy stood in the doorway, a robe wrapped around her, blue slippers on her feet.

"Hungry?" she asked.

"I could eat a southbound mule heading north," said Slocum.

"Sorry. All I have is pork bacon, biscuits, and beef gravy. Plenty of Arbuckle's."

Slocum grinned. "That'll do," he said, mounting the back porch steps. She embraced him strongly for several moments before she closed the door.

He sat at the table, sipping coffee, watching Amy move. Her hair was tousled and he could have sworn that she deliberately let her robe fall open every time she whirled away from the stove or counter to look at him. He saw her breasts, her firm long legs, the trim ankles, and between her legs, the thatch of dark hair that seemed to catch the light like dewdrops on grass.

The kitchen smelled of fresh-ground coffee, cinnamon, bacon, biscuits, and beef gravy simmering in an iron pot. It was nigh freezing outside, but here he was warm for a time, his senses still tingling from having made love with this good woman who hummed as she set plates on the table and looked at him with dipping eyelashes veiling her eyes. A coy breast peeked out at him as she set the steaming gravy pot on the table.

"Eat hearty," she said, as she set a crock filled with

fresh biscuits basking under a cloth dishtowel in front of him. "When you get back, I'll fix you a real breakfast."

And it hung there between them, in the silence, the thing neither of them wanted to talk about. He was going up there, and he might not be back. She brought the bacon to the table on a plate and it was crisp and thick the way he liked it. He looked down at it, afraid to look into her eyes too deeply.

13

Slocum did not ride through the town, but circled south of it, searching for a way up to the high valley that would not cross the regular trail. It was slow going, and treacherous. He followed several wrong paths before he found a game trail that would lead him behind the high ridge that shadowed the town.

It was hard slogging, going up the slope, and Slocum had to stop several times to wind his horse. But the game trail, for the most part, was swept smooth by wind, and gradually he crossed the roughest terrain and was able to reach the low end of the high valley. There he stopped for a smoke in the shelter of trees and reconnoitered. He had a good two hours ride before he would reach the place Dewey had told him about, but he would have protection all the way as long as he stayed within the treeline. He saw no telltale smoke in the leaden sky, but the wind burned his eyes, and the cold seared his face until he shrugged deeper into his coat and gave the horse its head. Blaze used the trees as shelter, picking his way around the deeper drifts.

Sometime before noon, Slocum stopped and munched on hardtack and jerky, washing it down with water from his canteen. In the silence, he heard men's voices—vague, discordant, disembodied sounds that floated through the valley like the echoes of ghosts. He was glad now that he had not built a fire. That Blackfoot could probably smell him as it was, and who else was out there looking for him? Unger, yes, and maybe one or two more. He thought he might have wounded one man, and he knew he had killed another. That left three, if his calculations were correct. Three against one. Maybe three against two, if he could find Ebenezer Lee in that vast empty land across the frozen valley sward.

The white glitter was blinding now that the sun was up higher, the light more evenly spread. Even though blocked by clouds, the sun was now another element Slocum had to consider. Its light distorted the landscape, and its reflection off the snow could cause temporary blindness. Once he crossed that immense flat, he knew, he would have to guard against glare and distortion if he was to reach his destination unscathed. If blinded, Unger and his men would have no more trouble with him than with a rabbit.

Slocum scanned the opposite slope as he wound his way through the trees, listening. Once he heard a horse whinny, but the sound could have come from any direction. The wind was shifting and the distance was so great that after the echoes had died down, he wondered if he had heard the sound in the first place. The mountains could play tricks on a man. They could fool him and taunt him and kill him.

Slocum shrugged off the melancholy that threatened to beset him. Sometimes, in that high country, a man alone became part of that great silence until he began to believe he would never see another human being again. Sometimes even the echo of a man's own voice could depress him even after only a few hours in the wilderness. Slocum supposed that was why men built towns and stayed together. Few could stand the loneliness, the emptiness of the West with its incredible vistas, its magnum of sky, its ancient rocks with their secrets.

He wondered that men did not use such wilderness to better purpose. If they did, Slocum was certain, there would be no quarrels, no fights, no wars such as the one he and Ned had come through. "Take any fightin' man," Ned used to say, "and put him in the mountains alone for a week, and that'll take all the hell out of him."

John chuckled to himself. Ned was right. The mountains had a way of bringing a man down to size. Every time Slocum began to think of himself as big, he had only to think of the Rockies and their awesome vastness to realize how very small he was, how puny man himself was in this great land.

Blaze whickered, perked his ears. Slocum leaned out of the saddle and put a calming hand on the animal's muzzle. "Steady, boy," he whispered.

He reined up and listened. In the silence, it seemed to him that he heard many sounds, but he knew this was only a quirk of the wind as it sang on the rimrock or bristled through the pines and firs and spruce trees. A man could hear bugles and voices and flutes in such a place, in such a wind. Even now, he almost thought he could hear the mournful baying of hounds back in Calhoun County, Georgia, the blueticks and redbones hot on the chase and the 'coon running for cover over the next hardwood ridge.

Slocum shook himself out of his dangerous reveries and tried to filter out the wind sounds, listen underneath and between for the true sounds of men, the deadly hunters who must be combing the woods for him even as he sat in his saddle, half-shivering in the mountain chill.

He heard nothing but the keen of the wind, the whick-whick of the pine needles dancing on branches overhead. He looked hard through the ghostly white woods, but saw nothing, only the flit of light and shadow on snow.

A snowy owl, roused from its somnolent perch on a spruce limb, flapped into sudden flight a few yards away. Blaze spooked and the owl veered, floated away on silent wings like a soundless spectre, disappeared before Slocum could bring Blaze out of his twisting struggle to gallop to safety. "Easy now, boy," he murmured, secretly glad for some break in the monotony.

He crossed the valley where it narrowed, not pushing his horse, but moving him steadily, on the least angle toward the other side. For the better part of an hour he was in the open, exposed, but he also knew that he had the advantage. He hunched over the saddle, one hand on his rifle butt, ready to bring it to shoulder at the first sign of trouble. As he increased the yardage, he began to feel better about the crossing, but he was not fully satisfied until he reached the cover of the trees. He stopped there, looked back across the icy flat, and wondered if he had been seen.

The morning wore on. Blaze stepped better along the narrow, windswept game trail that paralleled the eastern slope of the high ridge. Slocum's eyes burned from snowglare, but he relieved them by looking up through the trees, looking for the landmark Dewey Proctor had described to him.

There, finally, up a steep draw, he saw the big arrowhead. It was unmistakable, blazed on the rock face of the mountain as if etched there by some giant hand. He sucked in his breath, reined Blaze over on a heading that would take them to its craggy foot. Slocum wanted to shout for joy, but he knew he had riding to do, and there was no guarantee he would find Eb Lee. And if he found Lee, would he be alive?

* * *

Herb Unger looked at the frozen hulk that had once been Frank Gliddens. Red Sky had found him during the night, but this was the first time Unger had been able to piece together what had happened. Several yards away, the stiffened body of Dewey Proctor lay against the deadfall, his eyes closed, his hands folded across his middle.

Stan Loomis walked toward Herb, the deadfall at his back, his rifle loose in his mittened hand.

"This is where they holed up all right," he said. "Looks like Slocum got away clean. Tracks leading away was made the night before."

"Well," said Unger, "Red Sky should be back at any moment. We should know more by then."

"He got away clean," insisted Loomis, stubbornly.

"I know that, damn it! But where did the bastard go? Down the mountain? Back to town? Or is the son of a bitch still up here somewhere?"

As if in reply, the two men saw Red sky riding toward them from the west, his horse blowing twin jets of steam through its nostrils. The Blackfoot wore a scowl on his leathery face.

"Well?" Unger asked as Red Sky rode up and halted his horse.

"Him gone. Ride down mountain."

"Shit," said Unger. "He got two men." Dalbert Fricke had died during the night. It came as no surprise, but his moaning had kept them all up for most of the night. Dal had not died well. At the last, he was screaming in pain, and he fell into delirium, began babbling incoherently. Finally, Unger had put a gag in his mouth to shut him up. Fricke went into convulsions and died with bloody froth on his lips. "Two men, and then he lights a shuck for town."

"Him smart," said Red Sky.

"Maybe."

"I'd say he was smart," said Loomis, dangling his withered left hand. "We froze our balls off up here last night and that bastard was down in town stayin' warm, probably gittin' his bell-rope pulled by some filly."

"Shut up, Stan," said Unger. "I got to think."

"Think all you want," said Loomis curtly. "Man's gone."

Unger looked at the Indian. "What d'ya think, Sky? Think he'll be back?"

The Blackfoot nodded.

"I do too. He's a-lookin' for Lee and he ain't found him yet. I think them pitchpine torches was a signal. Now, Lee might have seen 'em, might not have. We got to figure out where Slocum and him's likely to meet."

"There," said Red Sky. He pointed toward the high valley and the ridge beyond that loomed up into the gray sky like a massive wall. "Him go there."

"Yeah, I think you're right," said Unger. "Well, we got plenty of supplies. Reckon we ought to split up, cover some territory? Loomis?"

"We got lots of country up here."

"Yeah. Well, if Slocum comes back, he'll be lookin' for Eb Lee, same as us. Reckon we ought to spread out and look for tracks."

"Better'n stayin' here and freezin' to death," grumbled Loomis, flapping his useless hand as if to ward off the chill.

"Well, then, mount up," Unger told Loomis. He grabbed up his own horse and climbed into the saddle. The place stank of death, and he did not look at the dead men again. Instead, he beckoned for Red Sky to follow him. They rode toward the high valley through the trees.

Later, when they split up, he gave orders for Loomis to circle the valley to the right, while Red Sky kept to the tree fringe to the left.

"I'll ride a line between you two. If anyone spots either Slocum or Lee, fire two quick shots and wait."

"You do not want us to follow Slocum and kill?" asked the Blackfoot.

Unger shook his head.

"That man's a handful. Better all of us go after him at once."

"Two shots," said Loomis, and rode off through the trees.

After Red Sky left, Unger doubled back and criss-crossed through the woods, looking for fresh sign. Somewhere, Lee was holed up, and unless he missed his guess, Slocum knew where he was. The trouble was, the mountains were so big they could swallow a man up. He was glad that Slocum had escaped, gone into town. That meant he would come back, and there wasn't a man in Silverado with balls enough to back him.

When Slocum returned to look for Ebenezer Lee, Unger knew, he would be alone.

Slocum rode for an hour up the draw, his green eyes scanning the snow for sign. Finally he saw the tracks, close to brush. He almost missed them, but a junco, flitting from a low branch, knocked off a peck of snow and drew Slocum's attention to the spot.

The tracks were old, filled in with blown snow. The rider had used the brush for cover, to conceal his horse's tracks. It was better than riding in the open. Not hard to spot, but not really easy, either. Whoever had made them had had full use of his senses. A good sign, if Eb Lee had ridden through here.

He followed the tracks. They wound through clumps of brush and over rock, and once he saw a spatter of blood on a mossy stone. It looked like a piece of rust, but it stood out against the white of the snow. Many hours old, he figured, like the hoof tracks themselves.

The tracks led him straight up the ravine to the sheer bluff just below timberline. There he saw the cave, the scars of fresh blast marks surrounding its gaping maw. Slocum shuddered, blew a stream of fog from his mouth as he exhaled. He dismounted, tied Blaze to a pine, gave the animal a handful of grain. He pulled his rifle from its scabbard and walked back into the open, just below the cave entrance.

He waded through hip-high drifts, saw the signs of another man's passage, not on horseback, but afoot. He saw more telltale splotches of dried blood and his pulse quickened.

By the time Slocum climbed up to the cave's entrance, his rifle was caked with snow, his trouser legs were wet, and his teeth rattled like marbles inside a cigar box. He brushed off the barrel of his rifle and checked the muzzle for snow. He rapped his trousers to shake off some of the freezing snow.

He listened for a long moment outside the cave, but he heard no sound.

Then he walked cautiously under the overhang and into the darkness of the cavern. His boots scuffed on dry land for the first time in days. The sound made a muffled echo off the walls. The air smelled dank, like old snow and water seepage, and as he peered into the black tunnel beyond, the hackles began to rise on the back of his neck.

"You take one more step, mister," said a voice, "and you're wolf meat."

Slocum froze.

14

Slocum swallowed hard, resisted the urge to bring his rifle up to cock it. For a long moment, he could feel his life hanging in the balance, teetering like an uncertain stone on the brink of eternity.

"If you're Ebenezer Lee, you got no quarrel with me," he said evenly. "I've come to help. The name's John Slocum."

There was a pause while the icicles dripped from the overhang and the seeping water plopped on the stone floor of the cave.

"Yeah, I'm Ebenezer. Ned said you was a-comin'. 'Bout time, too. Come on back real easy-like. I'm bad hurt, with a busted leg and the temper of a she-bear."

Slocum walked back into the tunnel, feeling his way. There was no shoring at that point, but the walls seemed solid. Then, he passed a slight bend, smelled wood-smoke, and saw a flickering glow some ten paces away. Weak sunlight spilled from an opening overhead, and there was a ladder leaning against the nearby wall.

Slocum approached. Eb Lee had the small fire covered with bushy cedar boughs so that the smoke broke up into thin wisps before it blew through the hole overhead and into the outside air.

Eb Lee lay next to the fire, his back propped against a buffalo blanket that was stacked next to the wall. Around him lay strewn cooking utensils, canned goods, rifle, ammunition, mining tools. Lee appeared to be in his mid-forties. He wore a beard, was balding under his rumpled felt hat. He was lean, with rugged features, strong wrists. He didn't look much like Jezebel, but he was a handsome enough man for all that. His blue eyes glittered in the light. The cave was warm, even with the smoke hole overhead.

"Set yourself, Slocum," said Lee. "How'd you find me?"

"Dewey Proctor."

"Dewey? Surprised. Not like him to give up secrets."

"He was dying."

"Shitfire," exclaimed Lee. "They jumped me two days ago. Unger, some of Carberry's trash. Big bastard name of Gliddens—Frank Gliddens, Dal Fricke, a pinch-faced son of a bitch, sneaky as a snake, and that Stan Loomis, got him a bum left hand, all withered up like a chunk of river driftwood."

"I don't know any of them but Unger. I think I put Gliddens's lamp out last night, after he killed Dewey."

"Damned shame about Dewey. Good man. So was Ned. Guess you heard he got kilt, too. They was about the only two left with gumption enough to stand up to that thievin', murderin' Carberry."

"I heard. I ran into your daughter during the storm, then I went into Silverado, where I met Proctor."

"You saw Jez. She all right?"

"Worried, but she's fine," said Slocum. "How about you?"

"Well, in that first jump, a rifle ball busted my shin. I cut it out, got some unguent into it, wrapped it up. I don't see no blue streaks goin' up my leg, but I got pain like a bad tooth."

"You got away."

"I gave 'em the slip. Unger, he tracked me plumb all over hell and gone after the others give up."

"Well, I figure he's still out there. The Indian, too, Red Sky."

"The damned Blackfoot. Well, I knew I couldn't hide from 'em forever. Sky will find me, likely. They'll pay pretty dear to get these old bones." He patted his pistol for emphasis. Slocum thought he was a pretty tough bird and was likely right. Whoever got to him first was liable to be the first to die. Eb Lee hadn't given up. He was wounded, but he had enough fire in his temperament to light a stove.

"Better let me take a look at that leg," said Slocum, laying his rifle down and slipping out of his coat.

"You look all you want, son. May have to cut it off."

Slocum scooted around the fire, saw the wounded leg jutting out straight. Lee had slit the trouser leg, had wrapped the wound in makeshift bandages made from bandannas and a shirt. Slocum started unwrapping it.

"I got some whiskey in my kit, case you need it. I may need a slug of it before we're through."

Slocum exposed the wound, touched the edge of it, where it was blue and puffed. Eb Lee's face drained of color and he passed out without a word.

The wound looked bad. The ball had struck it from an angle, coming in at the left side, tearing through the right shin. The exit hole was filled with splinters of bone, the flesh shredded up underneath like sawdust. He could find no gangrene, no evidence of poisonous gas bubbles under the nearby skin. But the wound needed cleaning out and packing.

Slocum drew his knife, placed it on a stone so that its blade jutted over the flames from the fire. Then he searched through Lee's possibles for the whiskey. He found a full quart of unlabeled liquid. He tasted it. It was whiskey, or something like it that was surely mixed with peppers, tobacco, and probably snakeskin. He poured some in Lee's wound, saw the wounded man wince. Then he took his knife, the blade heated through, the surface blackened by smoke, and began to trim the bone, cut through the mangled flesh. Beads of perspiration broke out on Lee's forehead, slicked his brows. He moaned and twisted in pain, but he did not awaken. Slocum staunched the bleeding with the hot knife, cauterized every blood seep.

Slocum moved the leg, saw that it was not actually broken. When it healed, it ought to work. He cleaned the wound again with another slosh of the bad whiskey, and then found the tin of unguent, and packed the bullet furrow. He didn't bandage it back up, but let it breathe. Likely it would heal faster. If it got to bleeding again, he could pack it with leaves and snow.

Slocum sat back on his haunches, exhausted. After a while, he put more wood on the fire, stretched out, and dozed. He wondered how long it would take Red Sky and the others to find his tracks coming across the valley, up this deep draw. He had no idea what time it was, but it had to be midafternoon. The light at the top of the cave gave him no idea of where the sun was, but he reckoned it had long since passed the meridian.

The cedar boughs began to smoke, so he stacked them higher, propped them up in a pyramid shape so they would break up the smoke but not catch fire. After a time, Eb stirred. Finally his eyes popped open, and he blinked at Slocum like a man suddenly brought up from the bottom of a well.

"Eh?" he grunted.

"Don't move too quick," said Slocum. "I didn't

cover up that wound, but it's got new packing."

Eb looked down at his shin, nodded. "Cleaned it up some, I see. It throbs, but it don't feel like it's goin' to fall off."

Slocum laughed. A man who could keep his sense of humor was a man to ride the river with, all right. But his brow knitted in concern. He looked at their skimpy supplies, thought of Blaze tied up outside. It would be best not to spend another night out in the cold. They could survive in the cave for a time, but if Unger and his bunch found them, it was only a matter of time before they got smoked out. Slocum was already feeling claustrophobic. He was not a man accustomed to being inside the earth for long periods of time.

"You thinkin' what I'm thinkin'?" Lee asked. Neither man had spoken for a good five minutes.

"We've got to get out of here," said Slocum.

"Well, it's ten miles down the mountain, and I got no horse. I run Blackie off, sent him back home."

"I know," said Slocum. "That's how I tracked you. Then I lost you and Unger started shooting at me."

Eb laughed, his eyes brimming with tears. Then the effort pained his leg and he had to stop.

"Haw! I led Herb a merry chase, I'll tell you. He didn't know whether to shit or go blind."

"I knew you were afoot, Lee. Looked to me like you climbed the mountain on your hands and knees."

"Oh, I scrambled around some, but maybe I used you to get away." Lee winked at Slocum, and suddenly it was clear to the tall man. When he had come upon Unger, Lee had taken advantage of the distraction and made good his escape.

"I see," said Slocum. "I suppose you saw the torches last night?"

"I did. No way I could get to 'em. I knew Dewey would find me if I didn't show up, so I just crawled back in here and gritted my teeth."

He was a wily bastard, Slocum thought. Like a fox. No wonder he was still alive, when Ned and Dewey were dead. Eb Lee was no fool. Slocum wondered, however, if either one of them would make it out of the valley now that Unger had the Blackfoot tracker.

"You think you can walk some?" Slocum asked.

"Some, I reckon. Before we get out of here, though, we better have a good look around. From that ledge outside, you can see a good ways. Want to take a look while I try and get to my feet?"

"I can help you."

"No, I want to try it on my own. If I fall down, you can pick me up or just leave me, dependin' on your disposition."

"I'll go take a look," said Slocum.

He got up, walked through the cave to the entrance. He stepped outside onto the ledge. Lee was right. He could see a long way, over the trees in the ravine and out onto the valley. It was a near-perfect defense position. But he couldn't see over the ledge atop him, and he knew there had to be another one there, a flat where the smoke hole was. And beyond that, what? More steep crags? Or could a man make his way down the ridge and come in behind the cave, drop down that smoke hole?

From where he stood, Slocum could not see his horse, but he knew the position where he had left him. He looked down, saw his tracks. They would be easy to find if any man rode up that ravine as he had done.

He saw nothing moving. The shining snow blinded him and after a few moments Slocum went back inside the cave. He found Eb leaning against the cave wall, his face bathed in sweat.

"You got to your feet," said Slocum.

"Yair, and I'm about to puke."

"Try to take a step."

"I already tried."

"Try again," Slocum urged.

Eb pushed away from the wall. His bad leg went out from under him. He crumpled and fell down. He doubled up in pain and Slocum went to him.

"You aren't going to walk out of here," he said.

"I reckon not," replied Lee.

"Take it easy. I'll think of something. We can't stay here."

Eb straightened out as Slocum stared up at the smoke hole.

"You see anybody?" Eb asked.

"No. But I left a lot of tracks coming in here. We'll have to move. And soon. Anyway, someone could come up behind us, drop down that hole."

"A mountain goat, maybe."

"A Blackfoot?"

"I reckon. You got worry on you, Slocum."

"We could hold 'em off for a while from the front," said Slocum. "But if they brought in more men, they could hold us siege, starve us out."

"They could. You a military man?"

"Was."

"Figured. What do you aim to do? I'm cripped up, and we couldn't last more'n a few days. We'd run out of water right quick, I reckon."

"You know, I saw some Indians travelin' once. They had some sick folks with them. They were Sioux, and they rigged these poles on their ponies. The ailing ones rode along pretty as you please. The poles were slender and rode over rocks easy. I could do the same for you."

"Rig a travvy? Yair, I heard of such."

"It'll take me time. I'll have to find some poles, cut 'em and lash 'em to the saddle, but I think it would work. We could get you home."

"I'm game," said Eb, wincing with a fresh shoot of pain as he moved his wounded leg. "The sooner the better."

"You have an axe or a hatchet?"

"Damn sure do. Got some rawhide strips in that canvas sack over yonder, too."

Slocum found the double-bladed axe and some wide rawhide strips, which he could cut into lashing thongs. Satisfied, he put on his jacket and strode toward the cave entrance.

"You hold on, Lee. I'll be back."

"Reckon I'll make us some soup and soften some hardtack whilst you're gone," said Eb. "Keep my mind on somethin' 'sides my busted leg."

Slocum grinned.

He found some slender aspens, cut two long ones down, and stripped them of branches. Each time he chopped, he listened. To him, the sound of the axe cutting into the wood sounded like thunder. By the time he had finished trimming the poles, he had worked himself into a sweat.

He lugged the two long poles over to where he had tied Blaze, crossed them at the thick ends, next to his saddlehorn. Taking the strips of rawhide, he slit them into manageable thongs, and lashed the two polls together. He knew he would need blankets or hides—the buffalo robe would do—to cover the frame he would lash to the slender ends of the two poles. By lashing these firmly, he could pull Eb behind him in comfort.

He went back to the aspen grove and cut several saplings to use for the frame of the bed. He trimmed them of bark, carried these back to the travois. He cut more rawhide strips, lashed the small saplings to the frame. Satisfied, he stepped back to survey his handiwork. A Sioux might do it better, but it would do.

He gave Blaze another handful of grain, picked up the axe and bundle of unused rawhide, and started back toward the cave. He scrambled up to the overhang, panting.

Gasping for breath, he paused.

Then he heard the distant crack of a rifle. He ducked, and a bullet thudded into the rock a foot from his head. Chunks of shattered stone stung his face. Slocum dove for the entrance as another rifle shot boomed. He crawled inside the cave.

Another rifle cracked and the bullet entered the cave, whined as it ricocheted off rock, caromed like a a mindless bat until it was spent.

"Slocum?"

"Yeah, Eb. We've got company."

Turning on his belly, Slocum looked out over the edge of the overhang. He saw the riders, then, three of them, on the flat.

In another hour, Unger and his men would be on top of them.

And there was only one way out—through the ravine. Slocum knew, before he even considered it, that he'd never get out in time.

15

Eb Lee was sitting up, his face drained of blood. Slocum looked down at the shin wound. It was bleeding slightly. Pain could take a lot out of a man, he knew, and Eb was just about at the end of his limit. Still, he didn't look like a quitter. He had his rifle across his lap, a determined set to his lips.

"What do you figure?" he asked Slocum.

"If they hurry, they'll be up here within the hour."

"They'll hurry. How many?"

"I saw three."

"We can hold 'em off."

"For how long? One man could pin us down here. We could kill one, and they'd still have one man who could ride for help."

"You always put sugar on your information?"

"We have to face what we have to face," said Slocum. There was no use pulling any punches. They were in a bad situation, and thinking it would be easy wouldn't get them out of it. "We'll have to hold them off for a while. Maybe until dark."

"Then what?"

"If they don't go after my horse, we might make it down there. I've got the travois poles rigged. I even know how I'm going to get you down there."

"One of 'em would be waitin' for us."

"You got any dynamite?"

"Yep. I got plenty. What you got in mind?"

"Just remember where it is. I'll need caps and fuses, too."

"Got 'em."

"I'll help you to the cave entrance. If you can shoot, I could use you and your rifle."

"I can shoot."

"Let's get to it, then," said Slocum. He helped Eb to his feet, gave him a shoulder to lean on. Then he half-pulled, half-dragged the wounded man to the cave entrance. He sat Lee down with a wall at his back, a few feet from the opening. There wouldn't be any more shooting for a while, and Slocum had much to do.

"Sit tight," he said. "I'll build us some defenses."

"Take your sweet time," smiled Eb, and Slocum chuckled. As long as a man could laugh at his predicament, nobody could count him out. He hurried, picked up boxes, tools, anything that would make a small barricade at the mine entrance. He figured he and Eb could lie out flat and shoot over it, expose the least amount of target to the outlaws. He dragged the buffalo robe out, too. He found the dynamite, fuses, caps, left them where they were, out of danger of being struck by a wild shot.

When he had built the low barricade at the lip of the overhang, Slocum helped Eb into position. Then he set out ammunition for both of them. Eb was shooting a Sharps .50 caliber carbine and he had about three hundred rounds of ammunition. Slocum had only about forty rounds for the Henry. The rest of his ammunition was in his saddlebags. He had twenty-five or so rounds for his pistol.

"Reckon they'll come straight at us?" Eb said, a slight quaver in his voice.

"No," said Slocum softly. "I figure they'll probe our defenses, test out our firepower. They'll pinpoint our positions, see how strong we are."

"You have any strategy?"

Again Slocum detected the quaver in the man's voice. He knew what it was. Men behaved in different ways before a battle. Some got scared and cried. Others got scared and prayed. They all got scared. Each man had to handle it in his own way. Eb was trying to put it out of his mind, but he'd already been shot once and he had the pain in his leg to remind him that bullets could not only hurt, they could kill. Eb was one of those who talked. He wanted to weigh his chances. He wanted to face it, not trust to luck or chance or prayer.

"Don't shoot unless you have a clear target. Let them find us. Let them make their moves. Nothing drives a man nuts worse'n not being able to hear or see an enemy."

"You know, eh?"

"I know," said Slocum. "We'll lie real quiet and listen. If they get too close, or their shots start getting too damned accurate, then we'll give 'em hell."

"I like your thinkin'," said Eb, and most of the quaver was gone.

Slocum had given it some thought. From the position of the cave, he knew they had the upper hand on the first strike. After that, three men could raise hob with their defenses. They could be flanked, even though the men on the flanks would face deadly exposure. A man coming straight up would have the least chance. He wouldn't be able to shoot until he was on the shelf of the cave itself, and by then it would be too late.

If he and Eb were still alive.

* * *

"What do you make of it, Herb?" asked Loomis, ramming fresh cartridges into his rifle's magazine.

"That was Slocum, all right."

"Hell, I never even saw the cave before now."

"Wouldn't have seen it if Slocum hadn't been moving."

Red Sky said nothing. He was the one who had spotted the man moving. He was the only one who hadn't shot at Slocum. The distance was too great, and all they had done was put the man on his guard. He said nothing now, but waited to see what Unger would do. Loomis was excited. He had fired the first shot.

"Yeah, I reckon," said Loomis, still staring at the image of the arrowhead. Because of the overhang, they could see only the top part of the cave entrance. To the naked eye, it looked like a black smudge. Only because Slocum had disappeared through it did they know, or suspect, that it was a cave.

"We'll have to go up there and smoke him out," said Unger.

"Hell, that's a long way off. That ravine is pure snow and thick brush."

"He made it up there," said Unger. "And I'll bet a day's pay Eb Lee is up there, too."

Red Sky sniffed the wind. He smelled woodsmoke, but again said nothing. He did not trust this Herb Unger so much. Two of Carberry's men were dead because he was a stupid man. Now they were tracking a man who was unlike the other miners they had killed. This one was a hunter, a killer. Slocum was a man he could like if they were on the same side, a man to respect. Unlike Loomis, the one with the shriveled hand, and Unger, the man whose temper made him foolish, Slocum was dangerous.

"Sky, you got any suggestions? We're goin' up there and do some serious shootin'."

"No," said the Blackfoot.

Unger frowned. He looked at Loomis, who shrugged.

"Hell, there's only two of 'em."

"They're in a cave," said Red Sky.

"That's right. Probably the silver mine. Hell, Carberry'll give us a bonus for this. We're going to be rich. All of us."

"Maybe," said Red Sky. He was not proud of himself. His people had long since given up their lands to live on reservations. He had taken to the white man's road and learned the ways of the white man's greed. But he was not proud of himself. He was an outcast from his own people and accepted only by the bad men of the whites. He had money and he could eat, but he had little else. Still, he could not change things. He had taken to this path, and he would ride it out. There was a sadness in him, however, because now he had seen a white man who was not afraid of the bad white men. This Slocum. It would be a great personal honor to kill him. But it was an honor that might not be granted.

"Let's get on up there," said Unger, finally. "We're wastin' time. We've got 'em holed up."

Loomis rode ahead. Unger held back to speak to Red Sky.

"You don't like this none, do you, Sky?"

"It is true, Unger. Two men in cave. Like cornered mountain lion."

"You scared of Slocum? Hell, he ain't but one man."

"Red Sky no afraid."

"Good. You just keep thinkin' that way."

Unger rode up behind Loomis, leaving Red Sky to read the tracks in the snow. He saw the blood and he knew it was not Slocum's blood. Maybe the white men would surrender, but he did not believe they would do this thing quick or easy. No, and if they did not kill Slocum and the miner, Lee, before nightfall, they would spend another night on the mountain. Red Sky did not like the night. It was full of spirits and there were three dead men already, their lifeless faces pointed upward, their sightless eyes staring at the sky.

Slocum cut several holes in the buffalo robe. Then he began cutting wide strips of rawhide, setting them alongside the robe.

"What are you doing?" Lee asked, lying in a prone position behind the barricade.

"I figure if we can hold them off until nightfall, I can get you out of here. This is a kind of blanket rig. I'll sew you inside the blanket, use the bigger straps for a shoulder harness. You can lie flat and I'll drag you down to the horse, put you on the travois."

"What if they find your horse?"

"Then I can pull you across country."

"Where?"

"To your cabin," said Slocum, as he continued with his makeshift rig.

"You don't know what you're getting into," said Lee.

"We can't stay up here. If we can hold them off until dark, we have a chance to get out."

Lee said nothing. Slocum didn't tell him that he thought their chances were slim as a Bull Durham cigarette paper.

When he had finished, Slocum took up a lookout

position behind the barricade. He moved when a dripping icicle spattered his nose. Lee laughed wryly, was immediately silent.

A twig cracked under a horse's hoof and the sound carried in the still air like a rifle shot. Lee twitched in shock. Slocum licked dry lips, set his rifle barrel atop the barricade.

"How close?" asked Lee.

"About half as far as you think it is," said Slocum. "They're close."

"Uh-huh."

Slocum looked down over the ledge, fixed his gaze at the farthest point, some eight hundred yards down the ravine. A moment later, he saw a dark shape fill the small opening. Then the shape turned and he saw that it was a horse and rider. Another man on horseback came into view, and the first man pointed up toward the cave. A few seconds later, the third man came through, and even from that distance, by the way he sat his horse, Slocum knew it was the Indian, Red Sky.

"What is it?" asked Lee. "See anything?"

"Three, so far." Then, after a few moments, he said, "I reckon there's just three."

"Bad enough."

"Unger and the Blackfoot. I don't know the other man, but he rides funny."

"Kind of side-saddle, one hand dangling over the pommel?"

Slocum squinted and nodded his head.

"That would be Loomis. Even with only one good hand he's a cold-eyed killer."

"Just sit tight."

He saw Unger point in his direction. Loomis looked up. Both men brought rifles to their shoulders. The

Blackfoot halted several yards behind the white men and sat motionless on his horse.

It seemed to Slocum that the Indian was staring directly into his eyes, but he knew that was not possible. The distance was too great. Even so, he had the feeling that the Blackfoot was calculating something far weightier than a long rifle shot.

Unger fired first. Slocum saw the flash of orange fire, then saw the cloud of white smoke mushroom from the rifle barrel. The bullet smashed into a row of icicles hanging overhead and sent a spray of ice down on top of him and Eb Lee. The shower of ice sounded like breaking glass inside the cave.

Lee ducked as a second shot, this one from Loomis's rifle, whizzed over their heads and smacked into the back wall of the cave, crumpling the lead, chipping off chunks of rock.

Lee started to rise up, return fire.

"Stay put," said Slocum. "No use wasting lead and powder. Let 'em wonder about us."

"Bastards," muttered Lee.

Slocum smiled. He peered over the edge of the barricade, saw two white men gesticulating to one another. The Indian still sat there, motionless, his horse under perfect control.

Finally, Unger and Loomis rode forward, followed by Red Sky. They came up the narrow defile, the two whites looking up toward the arrowhead. The Indian looked at the ground.

The riders disappeared for a time, reappeared later. They were much closer now. Slocum heard the disembodied sounds of their voices, punctuated by long periods of silence. He looked over the barricade, saw the three men split up.

His heart sank. The Indian, he knew, would be able to follow Slocum's tracks. He would find Blaze and the travois. He would know that this was their only means of escape.

A few moments later, more rifle shots exploded the silence. They were very close, but they could not see inside the cave. Slocum figured they could see the overhang, the top part of the cave. Bullets struck the ceiling, smashed icicles, caromed in all directions. The rifle fire was steady, deadly.

"God damn it, Slocum, aren't you going to shoot?" growled Lee.

"At what?"

"Damn, they're liable to kill us with bouncing lead if we don't do something."

"Let them think that," Slocum replied.

The hail of rattling lead was unnerving. The crack and whine of the bullets echoed in the cave's tunnel. Slocum felt a tug as one ball nicked his coat, a ricochet that snarled off two walls before slamming into a bank of snow near the cave entrance.

"Their gun barrels will get mighty hot pretty quick," said Slocum. "When they stop, I'll take a look."

He listened intently to the rapid shots. Still there were only two rifles firing. Where was the Indian? Why wasn't he shooting?

A few moments later, the firing stopped.

Slocum crawled up close to the barricade and slowly lifted his head.

He saw a flash of orange flame down to his left. He ducked, and the ball seared the air where his head had been. He swallowed hard, cocked his rifle, and poked the barrel over the barricade. He saw the man's shape in the trees, silhouetted against the stark white of the snow.

He took quick aim, held his breath, and squeezed the trigger. He heard the bullet hit home. Then he heard a man cry out. He saw him stiffen and stagger before going down.

"Damn it, Loomis!" shouted Unger.

Slocum looked at the fallen man in the snow. One withered hand twitched, then was still.

"You got him?" asked Lee.

"I got Loomis."

"Good. That leaves only two."

"Yeah, and I don't know where either one of them is," said Slocum.

It grew quiet and then Slocum began hearing noises in the brush down below.

The sun began to fall away toward the western horizon. It grew cold on the ledge outside the cave. Slocum shivered, hoped they could last until nightfall. Inside the cave, the fire burned down and the wind whistled through the smoke hole like some moaning mountain ghost.

16

The sound of a horse coming up the side of the mountain startled Slocum out of his reverie. He looked up, saw Blaze struggling up the steep slope, pulling the empty travois.

"What is it?" asked Eb.

"I don't know. A trick, I think."

He waited. The horse took one more step, then a rifle shot boomed in the stillness. To his horror, Slocum saw Blaze twitch and go down, his eyes wide with terror. Blood gushed from a belly wound. The horse staggered, tried to regain its feet and another shot rang out. The horse collapsed and began to roll over and over down the side of the mountain. Snow flew in all directions, brush cracked under its dead weight, and finally it slid to the bottom of the draw, a tangle of travois poles and lashing.

Slocum rose up on his elbows and readied his rifle. Anger blazed in his eyes, and his temples throbbed with the furious pounding of his own blood.

"Unger, you son of a bitch!" Slocum roared.

Deep laughter boomed from somewhere down the mountain.

"Slocum. You listen. You come down here. You and Eb Lee. We won't shoot you. You got to come unarmed. You hear me, Slocum?"

Slocum could almost see the man in his mind.

Unger. Standing there with his hands cupped over his mouth, shouting out his demands. A blind rage gripped Slocum, but he resisted the impulse to fire at the voice. He could see nothing, and if he remained where he was, Unger or the Blackfoot could pick him off. He ducked back of the barricade.

"What the hell happened out there?" asked Eb.

"That son of a bitch killed my horse."

"Deliberate?" Lee was incredulous.

"Deliberate."

"Now he wants us to surrender?" Lee asked.

"What do you think, Lee?"

"I think he'd shoot us as soon as we stood up."

Slocum laughed. He looked at Lee. Eb was no tenderfoot. The man had a lot of guts. Here he was, wounded, besieged, under fire, and he was cool and calm. He had seen men crack under less strain than they were under now. Yet Eb showed no signs of battle nerves or jumpiness.

"Well, Unger tried to force something there. He was a bastard to shoot my horse. That's worse than stealing."

"Yair," said Eb. "He should hang for that."

"If I get him in my sights, he'll never see that rope."

"Same here, Slocum. Now what?"

"I don't think Unger and the Blackfoot will rush us. They've burned a lot of powder and have nothing to show for it. I think they'll move in on us about dark, though."

"You think so?"

"I do. They won't want to spend another night in the open. They'll sneak in, rush us."

"We could take 'em," said Lee.

"We might, but we're not going to."

"You have a plan?"

"Not yet." Slocum rolled his lips together in thought. The killing of his horse presented a problem. Not an insurmountable one, but it added another factor to their slim chances of survival. A man on foot in the mountains was vulnerable. Eb Lee was worse off. He was wounded. He would slow them both down, so, for all practical purposes, Slocum was handicapped. A sound man alone might be able to slip past Unger and Red Sky. Two crippled men, however, would be easy prey. And, essentially, Slocum was just as crippled as Eb Lee, for he couldn't leave the man behind to be butchered by Carberry's men. Not and live with himself, he couldn't.

"This mine your silver claim?" he asked Eb after a while.

"Yep. There's a vein back there as wide as a barrel stave."

"That's what Carberry wants, you know."

"Carberry wants everything."

"Did you know that when he staked you?"

Eb shook his head. "I saw these rocks here. I knew they were rich. I couldn't see anything but the silver. His cash helped me find it."

"Now you know what's he's done," said Slocum.

"I couldn't figure a man like that out for a long time. It was hard to stomach, hearing that he had staked others only to move in on them when they made strikes. When I thought about it, it made some sense."

"Greed," said Slocum quietly.

"Yes. I've seen it before. Saw it in my own self. But Carberry's greed is the kind that eats a man up from inside. It's the kind that makes a man kill without any feelings about it. Carberry thinks he's better, smarter, more powerful than any of us who dig holes in the ground and kill ourselves on the rock. That's what makes him dangerous. He thinks he's beyond the law."

"Maybe he is."

"No, Slocum. There are laws and laws. He's not beyond the law that says a greedy man will finally go too far and someone will bring him down. Maybe another man more greedy, I don't know. Maybe someone like me. Or like you."

"Yeah," said Slocum with a sigh, "there is a law for such men."

"Colt's law," said Lee.

"Or Remington's," smiled Slocum, patting the butt of his pistol.

A rifle shot crashed through the silence. Both men ducked as the ball spanged off stone, rocketed shards of rock off their backs.

"Keeping us honest," said Slocum, but he saw the sun falling away over the mountains and he knew it would be dark soon.

Neither man spoke for several moments.

"Slocum," Lee said finally.

"Yeah?"

"You could make it if you left me here."

"I know."

"When it gets dark, you could slip out, get past them."

"They'd be on you in a minute, Lee. Forget it."

"Hell, you know I'd hold you back, even if I could limp on this bad leg."

"I've got an idea," Slocum said.

Lee looked at him, startled. "I hope it's a good one."

"It's the only one I've got," Slocum admitted. And, he thought, it might just work. If he could get everything ready, and if his timing was good, they just might have a chance to get away. He got up, stepped away from the entrance. He looked hard at Eb.

"You can start looking for a target now," he said softly. "If you see anything move down there, shoot it."

"Goddamn," grinned Eb.

Slocum laid out several sticks of dynamite. He cut the sticks in half. He then began cutting fuses into various lengths, trying to judge the time each one would burn. He embedded the powerful dynamite caps in the soft, nitro-glycerin-laced sawdust. He attached the fuses to the caps very carefully. He wasn't a powder man, but he had seen it done enough times to know what to do. He cut up six sticks, making twelve different grenades. Then, he put these in the side pockets of his coat, six on a side.

Next, he filled his saddlebags with all the grub he could find. When he was ready, he walked back out to the cave entrance.

It was dark outside. Slocum had let the fire die down, so that they would not be silhouetted.

"See anything?" he asked Lee.

"Nothing. You been at the dynamite."

Slocum looked down, saw the fuses sticking from his pockets. He grinned and nodded.

"Eb, I want you to crawl into that buffalo robe. I'm going to cinch it up and pull you down the mountain. You'll be helpless. Keep your knife handy and your gun ready. If I go down, cut yourself out."

"I guess I ain't got no choice."

"Not much. But I think I can drag you across the snow that way."

"Worth a try, I reckon."

Slocum was silent. He crawled to the barricade, looked over. The darkness continued to deepen. He saw the flicker of flame off to his left, knew what it was.

"Well, they're staying," he told Lee. "They've started a fire."

"I don't figure it," said Lee.

"They're waiting for us to make a break for it," said Slocum. "And that's just what we're going to do. Come on. I'll help you into that buffalo robe."

Slocum helped Eb over to the open robe. Lee moved his knife sheath around so that it was within reach. He slid his rifle alongside him. Slocum pulled the leather thongs tight and tied them. When he was finished, Eb, inside the robe, looked like a man in a cocoon, or a mummified human. Slocum suppressed the urge to laugh. He saw in Eb's face and eyes the abject look of helplessness.

"Here we go," said Slocum. He took a dynamite stick from his coat pocket, one with a two-minute fuse, fished a match out of his shirt pocket, and struck it on the cave wall. The match flared, released the acrid scent of burning sulphur. He touched the match to the fuse and saw it spew out sparks. He stepped to the overhang, drew back his arm, and threw the half-stick of dynamite as hard as he could, hurling it down toward the campfire in the trees. He did not wait to see the effect, but slipped into the harness he had made for the buffalo robe, picked up his rifle and saddlebags, and started walking off the ledge.

"We'll get out of here," he said to Eb. "Hold on."

Slocum slid, fell to his knees, then scrambled back onto his feet. He took a parallel track, searching in the dark for a clear path. The seconds ticked by as he waded through snow, pulling Eb behind him on the makeshift sled.

Behind him, the sled-robe skidded over the snow. Slocum felt the straps dig into his shoulders, but it was pulling fine. He made for a stand of trees, slipped among them. There he stopped and took out another stick of dynamite. He could not see the length of fuse, but at this point, it didn't matter. He struck a match on the receiver of his rifle and lit the fuse. He stepped out of the trees, hurled the dynamite overhanded toward the distant flicker of firelight.

Then he moved quickly, angling away from the fire and down the left side of the draw. It seemed an eternity before the first stick of dynamite blew. When it did, he threw himself forward and landed sprawling in the snow. The concussion smashed his ears. Stones and twigs shot by with the force of cannonballs, lethal debris hurtling through the trees.

He heard shouts and gunfire. He heard bullets spatter against the cave walls, chipping off bits and chunks of rock. Slocum lurched to his feet, felt his shoulders take up the slack in the leather sling.

The outlaws thought he and Eb were still in the cave.

Slocum hurried, lunging forward in great strides, pulling the robe sled behind him. It glided after him like a huge snake, hissing over the crusted snow. Slocum's trouser legs sogged with wet snow, but he forged on, and seconds later, the second stick of dynamite blew.

Again, Slocum hurled himself to the snow, covered the back of his head, as rocks and debris shot in all directions, clattering against the hillside. He would have liked to have seen the faces of Unger and Red Sky when those explosions went off. He regained his feet and slipped on down the draw, taking advantage of whatever confusion he had caused to make his escape. He heard shouts and curses, the scream of horses.

Then, more rifle shots, and these sounded closer to the cave. He had not hoped to have fooled Unger so, but he took advantage of it to gain ground in the darkness. He trudged on, the slope becoming steeper as he plunged through thick snow toward the flat.

It seemed like hours before he reached the edge of the valley. Slocum was soaked through with sweat, and every breath seemed to tear holes in his lungs. He stopped to rest and listen, walked back a few feet to check on Eb Lee.

He knelt down.

"Eb. You all right?" he whispered.

"Christ, Slocum. I think you broke every bone in my body. Didn't you see that goddamned rock back there?"

"No."

"I'm fine."

"We've got to cross this valley. Think we ought to take you home."

"No. Too dangerous. We've got to get to town, Slocum."

"Yeah, it's shorter."

"Not only that, but it'd be just like the cave if we go to the cabin. We'd be trapped there."

"I keep wondering about your daughter, Eb."

"Jez can take care of herself. You'd better hurry if you're going to get us out of here."

Panting, Slocum stood up. He looked out across the vast expanse of the valley. When a man was on horseback, it did not look so formidable. Now it seemed to stretch for miles. He knew, however, that it was not that far to walk. But it was across the open. There he would be most vulnerable.

He drew in deep breaths, adjusted his sling straps, and began the long trudge across the valley. Up on the mountain, up the ravine, he heard the boom of rifle shots, the angry whine of ricocheting bullets spanging off stone. The sounds were very comforting as he bent to the wind, heard the swish and hiss of the buffalo robe as it skidded atop the frozen snow.

Slocum forced himself not to look back, but to keep moving, a step at a time. He lengthened his stride, moved in a straight line toward the trees on the other side of the flat. Finally he realized how quiet it was. There was no more gunfire.

Well, he thought, *now they know.* If Unger and Red Sky had made it to the cave, they would know they had been, literally, buffaloed. He laughed wryly to himself. The Blackfoot would track them. It would take him a while, but he'd find the track, and once he knew what had made those swirls in the snow, he'd be down on Slocum like ugly on a bear.

Before that happened, Slocum knew, he had to make it across the treeless valley.

He looked over his shoulder, then, to see if he was being followed.

But all he saw, far up the draw, was the feeble flame of a fire flickering like some ghost light in the middle of a dark and forbidding wilderness.

He trudged on, wallowing through waist-high drifts, feeling the cut of the crust on his legs, the wetness of his trousers adding weight that dragged him down, sapped his strength. He looked up, and the treeline looked farther away than ever. It seemed he had been walking for hours. The sweat on his face began to freeze and the wind cut at his flesh like a razor.

He stopped dead in his tracks when he heard the eerie
shout from the ravine, sounding like a cry of a banshee
carrying on the wind.

"Slooooccummmmmm!"

17

In that cry, Slocum heard the anger and frustration of Herb Unger as he discovered that his quarry had escaped him. The sounds of that shout echoed through the hills, bouncing from rock to rock, from peak to peak, until they faded into nothingness. In the silence that followed, Slocum listened to the labored sound of his own breathing.

"Slocum," rasped Eb Lee, from the buffalo blanket.

"Yeah?"

"I don't have no feelin' in my back. I think it's froze solid."

"Can you make it down the mountain?"

"Yeah, I think so. It's only when you stop that I start thinkin' about it."

"Eb, we've got to get to Silverado. We can't stop anymore."

"You figure we can make it?"

"I can outwalk a horse in this snow. We'll make it."

"Good, son. You keep on goin'."

Slocum smiled in the darkness. He took up the slack, continued across the open expanse. When he looked up, the trees seemed much closer now, and he knew he had made good time. Unger and the Blackfoot were still up the draw. They would lose some time in picking up the track, but once they knew for sure where Slocum was headed, they might just forsake the trail. He was hoping they would stick to it, though. It was a hard way down for a man on horseback.

Once he reached the woods, the going became rougher. Now Slocum had to avoid fallen trees, thick brush. The stars appeared and he took his bearings. Fatigue slowed him down. His muscles began to ache, to cry out for oxygen in the thin altitude. He became dizzy, lightheaded, as he strained against the harness. Eb's weight seemed to grow. Finally, he could go on no longer without rest. He stopped, dropped to his knees. He wrestled out of the harness, staggered back to see how Eb was doing.

"Eb?"

"I'm alive. Barely."

"How's the leg?" Slocum panted.

"I don't even feel the pain. I'm numb all over."

"Better let me take a look at it."

"It's all right. Not bleeding. Slocum, you're plumb tuckered out."

"I am."

"There's a shortcut to town."

"Oh? You know where we are?"

"Yep. Been watchin' the stars."

Slocum let it sink in as he heaved, pulled in the thin air to starved lungs. He heard no sound but the wind and it had dropped off, except for minor gusts that rattled the snow on the trees. An owl floated by, ghostly in the starlight. When it beat its wings it barely made a sound.

"Slocum."

"Yeah?"

"Listen. You cut right about fifteen degrees. That'll bring you to an old flume just above the town. It ought to be packed with snow. It's straight down and we can slide for a good mile or so."

"Must be below the trail."

"It is. Ned Grover built it. He called his mine The Silver Lady. It's steep, but it'll save a lot of walking. We can make it in a half-hour. We get there, I can get out of this buffalo coffin and make it the rest of the way on my own."

"We'll have to go somewhere to hole up."

"I know. Got any ideas? Carberry's probably got men all over the place."

"The boarding house?"

"Good enough. Amy Nichols will take us in."

"She will," said Slocum, sure of it. God, he wished he was there now. He shivered at the thought of a fire and hot coffee, a shot of whiskey. He brushed the thoughts from his mind, took his bearings. He could see the stars through the trees. He marked one on a course fifteen degrees to his right. He didn't know which one it was, but it was bright enough to follow.

"I'm ready when you are," said Eb.

"Let's get to it."

Slocum slipped into harness again, oddly refreshed after the rest. It was still early, and they had made fair time despite the difficulty. It was still cold as hell, but now he knew he would not have to follow a three or four mile trail. He hoped he could find the flume in the dark.

Less than an hour later he crossed the trail and staggered to the edge of the steep slope. There, below, shining in the light of the moonrise, the flume stretched toward the base of the mountain. He could see the dim lights of Silverado spread out below him. His feet were numb, and he had been jumping at shadows for the past half-hour, but now he felt whole, exhilarated.

He heard rustlings from the buffalo sled, turned, and

saw Eb struggling to get out.

"Wait. I'll untie those thongs," said Slocum. He threw off the damnable harness, began to untie the thongs with numb fingers. Eb sat up and stretched.

"I've got feeling in my limbs," he said, "but not a hell of a lot."

Slocum laughed.

"It's not funny," said Eb.

"Better'n bein' dead," drawled Slocum. "We'll both sit on the buffalo robe and ride it down. We might get killed on the way down."

"Make a bobsled out of it."

"Yeah," said Slocum. He helped Eb to his feet, took his weight on his shoulder. He walked him over to the edge and sat him down. He went back for the robe, bundled it up, and carried it over to Eb, then dropped it in his lap. He looked down. They had about twenty feet to go before they hit the digging where the flume began. Underneath the snow, he knew, there would be tailings, and they could, possibly, cause an avalanche if they loosened the rock underneath. He said nothing to Lee about that, but just slipped around in front of him.

"I'm going to go down backwards, and pull you down after me. That way, if you slide too fast, I can catch you. Ready?"

"Ready," said Eb.

Slocum squatted and began to waddle backward. He pulled on Eb's boots, felt the man wince with pain. Then he began to slide on the snow, slowly. He dug in his heels, took it slow. Gradually, the two men made their way down the slope to the hole in the side of the mountain, a small opening Ned must have blasted to find his silver claim.

They reached the flume. Slocum hunkered down,

took the robe from Eb's lap. Eb held onto his rifle for dear life, looked back up the slope.

"What's the matter, Eb?"

"I thought I heard something."

"Well, if they came now, we'd be a couple of sitting ducks," said Slocum.

"You hear anything?"

"No. Come on. We'll ride sitting down. You get on the robe first, and I'll get behind you and push off."

But Slocum had heard something. A horse nickering, a tree branch cracking. If they stopped now, they would have no chance. If they could slide down the flume, they wouldn't have far to go. Hell, he could carry Eb to Mrs. Willoughby's boarding house, and do it at a run.

He settled Eb on the robe, climbed in behind him. He pushed off with his rifle, using it like a canoe paddle. Push, push, shove, and they were away, hurtling down the steep slide so fast the wind burned their faces, froze their eyes. Faster and faster they slid until the wind snatched their breaths away and flattened the flesh on their faces, made their eyes blur with stinging tears.

Eb shouted something, but Slocum couldn't hear. Eb's words were torn apart by the wind hurled past his ears like so much confetti, and still they continued their blinding rush to the bottom of the flume.

They shot out of the chute at the bottom and struck a snowbank, exploding it to white powder that turned into a silver spray in the starlight. Eb screamed. His cry was muffled as he crashed into a snowbank, overturned to fall face down in five feet of soft snow. Slocum dug in his heels, ground to a halt a few feet from where Lee lay sprawled.

Slowly, Slocum struggled to his feet. He shook the snow out of his collar, brushed powder off his rifle and coat. He hobbled over to Eb on unsteady feet, heard the miner splutter as he lifted his head out of the snow. He grabbed an arm, turned Lee over.

Eb's face was plastered with snow. He looked ridiculous, Slocum thought. Eb spat out a mouthful of snow, gulped in a breath of air like a man saved from drowning. He spluttered and coughed as Slocum helped him to his feet. Eb stood there on one leg, shaking his head. A chunk of snow fell from the brim of his hat.

The buffalo robe lay in a heap at the bottom of the slide, a sodden black lump against the bright white of the snow.

"Well, Eb? You want to go back up for another run?"

"No, I think that one trip'll do me for a while."

Both men laughed. Eb still clutched his rifle. It was caked with snow. He looked at it, slowly shook his head.

"Come on, let's get to the boarding house," said Slocum. "Feel up to it?"

"Mister, I'd rather walk than ride that goddamned flume again."

Slocum gave him a shoulder and the two men began the walk to town. People gawked at them in amazement as they trod the center of the street looking like a pair of snowmen come to life. A half hour later, they walked through the gate at Mrs. Willoughby's boarding house. Slocum knocked on the door.

Amy Nichols opened it. She was clad in a nightgown and wrap. Her eyes widened in surprise when she saw the two men standing there like tattered ghosts.

"John!" she exclaimed. "Is that you, Eb Lee?"

"It's us, and we need rooms," growled Eb. "Woman, I hope you got that fire stoked up. My skin is plumb froze to the bone."

"Yes, yes, come in, both of you. Oh, John, what happened? Eb, you're hurt." She shooed them in, closed the door. She helped Slocum get Eb to a chair, where they both undressed him. He snorted and fretted, shivered as Amy brushed snow from his face. She took his hat, removed his boots. She looked at the wound in his leg, but didn't even wince. Slocum gave her credit for that.

"John, you get out of those wet clothes. Let me tend to both of you. I'll get you some hot tea and—"

"Whiskey will do, Amy," said Eb. "Slocum, put another log on that fire before you get too comfortable. My blood is froze solid."

Amy and Slocum laughed. She went for the whiskey while Slocum stoked the fire and put more wood on. The flames danced, sparks flew up the chimney. He felt the warmth wash over him like a healing balm, warming his chilled bones.

Eb drank enough whiskey to thicken his tongue, and finally stopped shivering. Slocum drank sparingly. Amy heated up a hearty stew and the men ate like scavengers. She tended Eb's wound, put fresh dressings on it, and wrapped it lightly with gauze. Together she and Slocum got Eb to an empty room, put him to bed.

"I want to hear about everything that happened," she said, after they heard Eb snoring. She quietly closed the door.

"Do you want to hear it sitting down, standing up, or lying down?" he asked, an impish lilt to his voice.

"Lying down, John Slocum, as soon as you tell me what to do with those dynamite sticks in your coat."

"Oh, I forgot," he said sheepishly. "I'll take care of them."

"You know where my bedroom is," she said, a smile flitting on her lips.

"I can find it in the dark," he said.

"Hurry," she whispered.

Herb Unger looked at the tracks and swore. Down below he saw the dark shape at the bottom of the flume, knew by then what it was. He backed his horse away from the edge of the slope, rode back onto the trail. He turned the horse toward town. He knew he had another hour to ride. He had missed catching up to Slocum and Lee by no more than half an hour, he figured. Well, no matter. Both men were in town, and that was as good a place as any to put their lamps out.

An hour later, he sat in the living room of Carberry's house, telling him all that had happened.

"You get Dave Sanders and Willis Dorman," said Lucius, frowning. "Tomorrow. I want you three to hunt Slocum and Lee down."

"Oh, I don't think we'll have to do that, Lucius," said Unger.

"How's that?"

"When he finds out I'm in town, I reckon he'll come hunting both of us."

"Well, we'll be ready for him," said Carberry.

"And you'll have an ace in the hole, Lucius."

Carberry drew in a breath, took a cigar from the humidor on the table in front of the divan. His living room was wide and long, comfortable. Like other ambitious men, he had a huge desk, the most prominent piece of furniture in the room. He and Unger drank good whiskey from thick glass tumblers.

Carberry bit off the end of his cigar, spat the butt out

into a clay ashtray as he fished for a match in his vest pocket.

"Yeah, if Red Sky gets back in time," Carberry said wryly.

"He will," said Unger, smirking in satisfaction.

Carberry lit his cigar, blew a plume of blue smoke into the air.

"He'd better," he said softly.

Jezebel heard the horses nicker, and ran to the front window. She peered out into the darkness, but could see nothing but moonlit snow and shadows. She listened, heard the cabin tick with silence.

She strained her eyes, heard her heart beat wildly.

Oh Pa, she thought, *I hope you're out there, coming home.*

Her heart leaped into her throat when she heard the sound of the back door opening. She gave a little cry, turned from the window.

She started across the room, when the shape filled the hall doorway.

Red Sky stood there, a rifle in his hand, staring at her with expressionless eyes.

Jezebel's hand clutched at her throat. The blood drained from her face and her knees turned to jelly.

"Get coat," said the Blackfoot. "You come."

"Leave me alone," she whimpered. "Get away. Get out of here."

The Indian stalked toward her, and she backed up until she struck the front door. Her eyes rolled in their sockets.

She opened her mouth to scream. Red Sky's lips curled back, revealing his teeth.

"You yell," he gruffed. "No one hear."

"Don't touch me," she pleaded as she cringed, trying to get away from him.

"You come now," he said. "See father."

"You—you're lying. Get away from me."

Red Sky brought the rifle up, aimed the butt at the top of her head.

She screamed one last time.

18

Slocum heard the voice, but could not make sense of the words. The sound seemed to be swathed in cotton, the words garbled. In the dream, they didn't make sense, and yet the urgency scattered his thoughts, scrambled them in the darkness of sleep like objects tossed awry by a Georgia hurricane.

"John, wake up, wake up!" Amy shouted.

Slocum felt someone shaking him as he swam upward from the dark seas of sleep. He seemed caught in cobwebs, the strands as hard and tempered as steel. His brain was filled with them, with a deep fog that would not disperse.

"John Slocum. You wake up this minute!"

Slocum heard the sharp words clearly, opened his eyes, blinked at the harsh light of morning. Amy Nichols stood at the edge of the bed, leaning over him. Her face wore an expression of urgency, exasperation.

"Huh? Where am I?" he mumbled.

"John, you've got to listen. It's important. Are you awake?"

He tried to sit up and brush the cobwebs out of his mind. He took in his surroundings, realized where he was. He and Amy had made love the night before. He reeked still of her musk, and he didn't remember falling asleep. He shook his head, dispelling the last chains of sleep that had drugged him, clearing his head.

Amy was fully dressed, wearing a patterned frock with a high bodice and full sleeves. It came to him then that she was probably on her way to work and he had overslept.

"Yeah, I'm awake. I must have really been under. What's the matter?"

"Someone came to the house a few minutes ago. From town. It was a couple of women who visit Mrs. Willoughby every week. They said there was a lot of talk."

"Talk? What talk?"

"Herb Unger came riding in last night. Said you killed some men. He said he was going to kill you, John."

"What about the Blackfoot?"

"I didn't hear anything about him." She sat on the edge of the bed. Worry lines furrowed her brow as she took his hand in hers. "Oh, John, I'm scared. Carberry's probably going to try to kill you and Eb."

Slocum scrambled out of bed.

"Thanks, Amy. Don't worry." He hopped around, looking for his clothes. Amy brought them from the closet where she had hung them up. He dressed while he listened to her instructions.

"There's coffee made, and biscuits, and—"

"Coffee's fine. I don't have much appetite." He pulled on his boots, stood up, and strapped on his gun-belt.

"I have to go to work," she said. "Please stay here, John. I'll try to get help."

"No," he said. "I've got to face Carberry down. Eb still asleep?"

"Yes. He—he's in no condition to . . ."

"I know. He'd just be in my way."

She looked at him as if he had just lost his mind.

Her eyes widened in a look of credulity and she pursed her lips as if trying to form the first word of a stern reprimand.

"John, you're not serious. You can't face those men alone."

"Who am I facing?" he asked evenly.

"I—I don't know. Lucius, Herb Unger, maybe Dave Sanders. And there's Willie Dorman, he's another of that bunch."

"Four men. Maybe five, if the Indian came back."

"You can't do it, John."

"I can't wait for Carberry to come after me, either."

He strode toward the door. She blocked his way. He took her in his arms, kissed her hard on the lips.

"John," she sighed, and he heard her start to whimper.

"Go to work," he said. "I'll see you later, maybe."

He pushed her aside. She came after him.

"Just like that. John, you—you can't go into town. I—I won't let you."

He went to the kitchen, poured some coffee. Upstairs, he heard the sound of women's voices, chairs scraping on the floor. That would be Mrs. Willoughby and her visitors, he thought. He heard the tinkle of china, laughter.

"Amy, I'm not going to argue with you. Don't worry, I won't just walk into trouble."

"Well, I can't help it. I am worried. John, please let me think of something. Let me try to get help."

"Go to work, Amy. I've got to think."

She glared at him, doubled her hands into tiny fists that she plunked down on each hip. She puckered up her mouth and blew air out through her nose.

"Oh, you!" she exclaimed, and twirled around on her feet and stomped back through the house. A few moments later, he heard her call up the stairs to Mrs. Willoughby, saying goodbye. He heard the front door slam. It jarred the whole house.

Slocum sat down at the kitchen table and sipped at his coffee. He felt good after a fair night's sleep. Outside, he heard a rooster crow, the yap of a dog. Unger would want to call him out. He and Carberry had some kind of a plan, probably. Whatever it was, it wouldn't be fair. He couldn't expect any quarter to be given. Nor would he show Carberry or any of his men the slightest mercy.

He knew he could expect no help from the townsmen, either. Unger had apparently already spread his poison, his lies. He was making Slocum out to be a cold-blooded murderer.

Slocum finished his coffee and retrieved his coat from the closet. He stuffed the pockets with the remaining sticks of dynamite he had stored on the back porch, then walked through the house one last time. He checked his pistol, took his rifle in hand. He was ready.

As he opened the front door, he heard footsteps on the stairs. He turned, saw two ladies descending. They saw him at the same time.

"Oh," said one. "You must be the one they're talking about in town."

"I wouldn't know that," said Slocum.

"Clare, be quiet," said the smaller of the two women. Slocum figured they were in their late fifties, at least.

"I won't, Henrietta. This young man is in grave danger."

Slocum smiled.

"I wouldn't go into town if I were you ladies," he said. "There's liable to be trouble. People hurt."

"You're going after that awful Mr. Carberry, aren't you, sir?" asked the one called Clare.

"Yes, ma'am."

"Well, you won't get any help from the miners."

"Didn't expect any," said Slocum. "But I am curious. Why?"

"Why, didn't Amy tell you? Mr. Carberry is saying that you killed Dewey Proctor in cold blood."

Slocum's jaw hardened. A muscle twitched along the bone. "No, ma'am. She didn't tell me."

"Amy says you didn't shoot Mr. Proctor," said Clare, as Henrietta tugged at her arm. "And I believe her."

"No'm, I didn't kill Dewey."

"There, Henrietta! See? I told you Lucius Carberry was a liar and a no-account."

"Oh, Clare!"

Slocum opened the door and stepped through it.

"Mr. Slocum?" called Clare. "That is your name, isn't it?"

"Yes."

"What are you going to do about Lucius Carberry?"

'I'm going to kill him," said Slocum.

The two women gasped and shrank close to one another. Slocum smiled and closed the door.

People stared at Slocum as he walked down the street, his boots ringing on the frozen ice and mud. The overcast sky hung low over the town. Slocum's breath turned to smoke in the chill morning air. It was a hell of a day to die, he thought.

19

Slocum walked down Main Street, stopped in at a store that sold tobacco. The man at the counter seemed nervous.

"A cigar," said Slocum, digging into his pocket for money.

"Just one? What kind?"

"Just one. A cheroot will do."

"I—I have cheroots. Yes, sir."

"I'm looking for a man named Unger," said Slocum as he took the cheroot from the man's trembling fingers.

The storekeeper made change out of a cigar box, gave the coins to Slocum.

"Unger? I—I reckon he's at the saloon. Most ever'one is."

Slocum stuffed his change in his pocket, stuck the cheroot in his mouth. "Thanks," he said.

Down the street, he could see men's heads poke out, then pop back into doorways. There wasn't a soul outside on the shovel-scraped boardwalks. Heaps of dirty snow lined the street. They looked like graves, bleakly rowed up on both sides of Main.

There were horses and mules tied to the hitchrail outside the Silverado Saloon. Men stood in the doorway. As Slocum approached, they disappeared. Slocum saw faces floating behind the glass in the general store, and he knew one of them was Amy's. He looked only at the saloon now as he left the center of the street, strode toward the door at an angle.

Slocum didn't recognize any of the horses. He stepped up to the door, waited for a few seconds. Inside he heard whispered conversations, nervous coughs, the scrape of chairs. He could smell the woodsmoke, the tangy aroma of beer and whiskey. A glass tinkled like a single piano note.

Slocum kicked the door opened, waited for a shot as he ducked back to the side.

"Unger? You in there?" Slocum shouted, holding his rifle at the ready.

"I'm in here, Slocum."

"Tell everybody to get out."

"That's up to them, Slocum."

"First man I see I'm going to shoot down."

There was a collective gasp, and men began streaming from the saloon. Slocum watched them scatter in the street like chickens. Some untied their horses and mules and rode down the street, coats flapping.

One man stepped to the side, looked at Slocum.

"He ain't alone," he said.

"How many?" asked Slocum.

"Him and Willis Dorman. Dorman's at the bar, Unger's settin' behind a table way over to the right."

"Thanks," said Slocum.

"They got Greeners," said the man as he tipped his hat.

"You better clear out," Slocum told him.

"Just one thing, Mister."

"What's that?"

"Did you kill Dewey like they said you did?"

"No. Unger killed him."

"Just what I was a-tellin' ever'body." The man

grinned wide and walked away from the saloon. Slocum waited as the man took cover behind a post on the opposite side of the street. It was quiet inside the saloon.

"Well, Slocum? You comin' in?" bellowed Herb Unger.

Slocum said nothing.

He knew his chances were not good. Likely, Unger and Dorman had double-barreled shotguns cocked and aimed at the door. It would be suicide to walk in there. He would look like a sieve before he could take a breath.

Calmly, Slocum lit the cheroot with a sulphur match. He puffed until the tip glowed cherry red, then dug out a stick of dynamite with a two-minute fuse.

"Unger. You remember what happened last night?"

"I don't get you, Slocum."

"The dynamite. Here's a reminder."

Slocum touched the tip of the cheroot to the fuse. When it hissed, he tossed the dynamite through the open door of the saloon. He counted the seconds.

"Goddamn!" shouted Dorman. "That son of a bitch threw a stick of dynamite in here!"

"Run!" shouted Unger.

Slocum cocked the rifle.

Ten seconds later, Slocum ducked, dashed inside the saloon. He ran to his left, saw the man at the bar raise the Greener to his shoulder. Slocum fired from the hip, saw the bullet smack dust from the man's coat right over his heart.

Dorman twitched, and his fingers squeezed both triggers of the shotgun. As he fell back against the bar, the twin barrels swung upward. Exploding powder spewed fire and smoke, double-ought buckshot into the ceiling, knocking loose chunks of plaster and wood, showering

Slocum with dust and rubble.

Dorman slid sickeningly down the front of the bar, his head cocked at a crazy angle, his eyes staring sightless into empty space. Ten feet away, the dynamite fuse hissed like a snake, spitting out glowing sparks like a miniature volcanic eruption.

Slocum crabbed to the edge of the bar, cocking his Henry rifle, as he swung to cover Unger in the far corner of the room. Unger stood there for a moment, undecided. He looked at the stick of dynamite, then at Slocum.

"Drop it, Unger," Slocum said.

"Christ, Slocum, we'll be blown to pieces."

"Put that shotgun down. I can put out the fuse. You're too far away."

"Damn you, Slocum." Unger's face contorted in rage, and he brought the Greener up to his waist, leveled it at Slocum. John fired the rifle, got to his feet before the smoke had cleared. He saw Unger spin away, grab his left shoulder. The shotgun flew from his hands and smashed through the window.

Slocum raced to the stick of dynamite, stepped on the burning fuse. He stomped it dead, ground the sparks into the floor. Sweat poured down his face, oiling it to a high sheen. The fuse had less than thirty seconds of burning time left.

Unger's right hand darted for the pistol at his belt. Slocum saw the move, but knew he could not cock the rifle in time. He dropped the Henry. His hand streaked for the gun on his hip. Unger was fast. Very fast. His hand blurred as he grasped the handle of his Colt. Slocum saw Unger's hand jerk the weapon free of the holster, saw the pistol barrel come up, come up, clear the leather as Unger went into a fighting crouch.

Each second seemed an eternity as the two men faced each other. Slocum didn't think. He didn't measure the fractions of seconds. His hand closed around the grip of his pistol, his finger groped for the trigger as his thumb came down on the hammer. He cocked on the rise, cleared the holster, tilted the pistol, and fired. Unger's shot blast boomed at virtually the same time, and the room filled with white clouds of smoke.

Slocum twisted on one boot heel, cocked again as he brought his pistol up level. He was not sure whether his bullet had struck home. But he felt a tug at the sleeve of his coat, heard the sheepskin rip as Unger's bullet sped harmlessly by him.

Slocum brought his pistol up level, strained to see through the smoke. His ears hurt from the explosions. The acrid smoke assailed his nostrils, gagged him. He saw Unger stagger toward him, his pistol held out at full length. Unger's thumb pressed on the hammer of the Colt.

Slocum didn't wait, but fired pointblank at Unger's chest. Just before he squeezed the trigger, he saw the dark hole in Unger's left shoulder. Blood pumped through it with every beat of his heart. The .44 bucked in Slocum's hand and he saw his bullet tear another hole in the center of Unger's chest. Then the smoke billowed up and obscured his vision. Powder blowback stung Slocum's face.

Unger twisted backward, danced horribly for a split-second like a berserk marionette, then crashed into a table, knocking it sideways as he fell headlong and pitched to the floor like a dead weight. His Colt fell from his fingers as Slocum stepped up to him, a plume of smoke curling up from his gun barrel. He put a boot beneath Unger's belly and flipped him over.

Unger looked up at him with rheumy eyes, his mouth slack and open. A trickle of blood seeped up over his lips, dribbled down his chin. The two holes in his chest oozed freshets of blood and foam. Unger's mouth moved, like a gasping fish.

"Satisfied, Unger? You don't have much time. Where's your friend, Carberry?"

"Slocum," rasped the dying man, "Carberry's got Jezebel Lee. Sky brought her in this—this morning."

Slocum's blood froze. He saw the hatred in Unger's eyes. Even though he was dying, the man's hate still burned inside him. More blood bubbled out of his mouth, and some of it was pink, and some full of lung air.

"You're a liar, Unger."

"You see—Carberry. He—he's got the girl. He'll kill her, too."

Slocum believed him.

Anger began to flood his senses as he looked down at Unger's face, the glittering eyes full of senseless fury. The blood pumped faster now, poured from the hole in his lung. Slocum felt no pity for the man. He had called this end down on himself.

"Th-there's no law in Silverado," Unger gasped. Then his eyes turned frost and he choked on blood, began to cough. The paroxysm seemed to last a long time as Slocum stood there, watching him die. But Unger held on to that slim thread of life and he stared up at his killer with glazed eyes that still flared with the burning hatred inside him.

"There may not be any law in Silverado, Unger," said Slocum, "but, by God, I mean to see that there's justice."

"You—you'll die, too, Slocum."

Slocum could think of only one thing. Carberry and the Blackfoot had Jezebel Lee. He was quite sure that Carberry would not hesitate to kill her if it would save his own skin. He had to save her somehow, and put Carberry down once and for all.

He knelt down beside Unger.

"Where's Carberry?" he asked.

Unger seemed to reach down inside himself, draw air into his one good lung.

"Office," he said. "Waiting."

Slocum stood up. Unger was a hard man to kill. He wasn't dying easy. Sometimes a lung-shot man could live a long time. He wanted to put a bullet in the man's brain, erase him from the face of the earth. But it was hard to kill a man like that. In the heat of battle, a man didn't think about such things, but up close, without anger or fear in the blood, it was damned hard to pull that final trigger.

Unger coughed once more. Blood gushed from his mouth and no air came back in. He twitched once, then his eyes dulled and went dark.

Slocum picked up his rifle and the stick of dynamite, and walked to the door.

"See you in Hell, Unger," he said.

20

Slocum stepped out of the Silverado Saloon, leaned his rifle against the wall. He looked up and down the street as he reloaded both the pistol and the Henry. His jaw muscles clamped the cheroot firmly in his jaw. His eyes glittered dangerously. Across the street he saw the man he had spoken to earlier. He and several others were talking and pointing in his direction. Several people emerged from the general store, and he saw Amy rushing toward him, passing through the pack. Then the cluster of men who had been in the saloon broke up and headed his way.

"John," exclaimed Amy, rushing up to him ahead of the others, "are you—are you all right?"

"I'm fine," he said.

"Slocum," said a miner, "there were two of Carberry's men in that saloon. They go out the back?"

"No," said Slocum.

"Well, where are they?" asked another man. "We saw Herb Unger and Willis Dorman settin' in there waitin', jest a-waitin' fer trouble."

"They found it," said Slocum, jerking his thumb over his shoulder.

The crowd seemed aghast as they muttered among themselves. Slocum stepped down, pulled Amy close.

"Carberry's got Eb's daughter, Jezebel," he whispered.

"Oh, no," she gasped. "Poor Jez."

"The Indian brought her in. I'm going over to Carberry's now."

"John," she said, "you can't go over there alone. Don't you see? That's what he wants."

"I know."

"He—he sent those two in the saloon after you, John. I heard them talking while you were in there."

"I know that, too."

"But, if Lucius didn't come with them, that means he's at his office just waiting for you. He and that Indian and probably Dave Sanders. I saw him riding over to Montana Mining when I came in this morning."

Slocum pulled on Amy's arm and led her away from the group. Some of the men went inside the saloon. He heard them exclaiming over their finds. Others went to spread the news of the gunfight. It would be all over town before Slocum could face down Carberry. There was no getting around that, though. Human nature was a hard thing to go up against.

"Amy," said Slocum, "I don't know what Carberry's got up his sleeve. I know he's got Jezebel and he's using her as an ace in the hole. Now he'll know that Unger and Dorman are dead."

"And that you killed them," said Amy.

"Right. So Jezebel is in real danger now. He may kill her the minute I show up." He shifted the cheroot in his mouth. It had gone out several moments ago during the gunfight and he hadn't noticed it.

"That's just why you shouldn't go over to Carberry's office alone."

He stepped away from her, looked down his nose, and cocked his head slightly to one side.

"How many men did you talk to this morning about helping me?" he asked.

"Why, quite a few," she said. "It was all over town that there was going to be trouble, that you . . ."

She stopped speaking, realizing that John Slocum had made his point without uttering a word.

"But, John, that still doesn't . . ."

"Amy," he said solemnly, "I want you to go back over to that store and stay there. I don't want you to even think about what I'm going to do. You'll hear a ruckus, likely, and when it quiets down, you come on over to Carberry's office. If I'm still alive, I'll give you a peck on the cheek and a pat on the behind. If I'm not, say a prayer for me." He grinned and took the cheroot out of his mouth, eyed it before fishing out a sulphur match from his pocket. He struck the match on his pistol butt, lit the cheroot again.

"John . . ."

"Don't say another word, Amy. Don't even think about what might happen."

"Do you—do you know how you're going to free Jezebel?" she asked timidly.

He blew a spool of smoke into the air, removed the cheroot, leaned over, and gave Amy a peck on the cheek.

"That's on account," he said, with a broad smile. "And, to answer your question, no. I'm just going over to that phony mining company and open the ball." He patted the dynamite sticks in his pocket, then strode away, leaving Amy standing there more bewildered than ever.

* * *

Here and there, Slocum saw men peering at him from between buildings. Some stood at upstairs windows. Others lazed in doorways, watching him as he strode by, puffing on the thin cigar, looking like a man going to a card game instead of to a deadly confrontation with Lucius Carberry.

But they all knew. They looked at Slocum as if he was a man striding to his own funeral, a man gone plumb loco.

"Good luck," someone said.

"Watch yourself," said another.

Slocum walked through an invisible gauntlet, wondering if he would ever walk back the same way. He saw the office down the street and continued toward it, his concentration intense now, the cheroot in his mouth, glowing red-hot at the tip.

The office seemed deserted as he halted a few yards away, looked at the weak sunlight shimmering on the plate-glass windows. He stood there for a moment, then lifted his rifle, worked the lever. The sound of the mechanism carried up and down the street. People shrank back in the doorways and from the windows. The sound was very loud.

He walked up to the door of the mining company and twisted the handle. The door creaked open.

"Come on in, Slocum," said Carberry. "I've been expecting you."

Slocum poked the barrel of the Henry through the door first, edged through behind it, his finger firm on the trigger.

Carberry stood there with a smirk on his face. He was armed, but his hands were empty. He wore a sixgun in a holster and had another pistol jutting out of his belt.

"Slocum," said the outlaw, "you put away some good men, but it's all over for you. Put down that rifle real slow, or Jezebel Lee won't draw another breath. You see, I always get what I want."

Slocum looked at Carberry with steely eyes that bristled with green fire.

"Where is she?" he demanded.

"You want to see her? Sure."

Carberry snapped his fingers, and Slocum almost shot him because of his arrogance, but he held off, knowing the hand had to be played out.

The door to the inner office opened and two men came out, dragging Jezebel between them. They had their pistols in their hands, and the muzzles were pressed up against both sides of Jezebel's head.

"John, oh John," she stammered. "I—I'm so sorry."

"Shut up!" Carberry boomed.

Slocum looked at the Indian first. Red Sky looked at him, too, his dark eyes hard in their sockets, his face impassive, expressionless. A look passed between them. The other man he took to be Dave Sanders. He was a squint-eyed man who wore horn-rimmed spectacles. A pair of faded red suspenders held up his trousers. He was pot-bellied and balding, with a thin scar just above his upper lip. He had the cold pale blue eyes of a killer. His finger curled around the trigger of his pistol as if he was ready to squeeze it on his own.

"You see?" said Carberry. "One bad move from you, and they'll blow that woman's head clean off her shoulders."

Carberry nodded, and both men thumbed back the hammers of their pistols. The sound was ominous in the interval of silence. Jezebel's face paled and her eyes widened in fear. Slocum looked at her out of the corner of his eye, saw that her hair was tousled, and she had a lump on the side of her head, a bruise on her cheek. The anger boiled in him, but he quelled it, held the rifle steady, aimed at Carberry's gut.

It appeared, to each man there, Slocum included, that it was all over. Slocum had lost.

"Give it up, Slocum," Carberry said slowly. "That gal's just a hairtrigger away from eternity."

"Please don't let them kill me, John," Jezebel pleaded. Her words wrenched Slocum's heart.

"No, I won't do that," said Slocum, dejectedly.

"Lay the rifle down, Slocum. Real slow," said Carberry.

Slocum stooped, set the rifle down. When he came back up, his hand went into his coat pocket, pulled out the stick of dynamite with the short fuse. He concealed its shape with his hand.

"What's that you've got there?" demanded Carberry. "No tricks."

Slocum brought the dynamite up to the cheroot, held the fuse a scant fraction of an inch away from the glowing tip.

"If you don't turn Jezebel loose right now," Slocum said with deadly calm, "I'll blow us all to kingdom come."

He puffed hard on the cigar and moved the fuse still closer to the pulsating flame. Carberry's face drained of color. Sanders's mouth went slack. Red Sky's eyes narrowed to slits.

"You—you're bluffing," stammered Carberry.

"I don't bluff."

Carberry looked over at the Blackfoot.

"Sky? What do you think? Will he do it?"

Red Sky nodded.

"This fuse will burn down to the cap in about twenty-five seconds," said Slocum.

Dave Sanders spoke for the first time.

"Boss," he said, "he's right about that fuse. I give it less than twenty seconds. I do know this jasper's makin' me mighty spooky."

"So, you gonna let him bluff us with that?" asked Carberry. "We can kill the woman, drop Slocum, and toss that stick outside in less than ten seconds."

"You'd have to throw it two hundred yards," said Sanders, "or your head would explode like a ripe gourd."

Slocum could see that he had them on the fence. He could wait no longer to make his move. He jabbed the fuse into the end of the cigar. The fuse caught, began spewing sparks, hissing like an adder.

For a moment, the outlaws froze as they watched the fuse burn in hypnotic fascination. Then Slocum put the dynamite on the floor between his legs. He looked at Carberry and smiled calmly.

"Shit!" exclaimed Sanders, and bolted for the door.

Red Sky shoved Jezebel down and started to race after Sanders. She hit the floor sprawling as Slocum went into a crouch.

He drew his pistol, thumbed the hammer back, and the gun bucked twice in his hand as he fanned the hammer. Sanders pitched through the door, a bullet blowing out two ribs and a chunk of lung before it ripped into the kidney and exited under his left armpit.

Red Sky went down like a poleaxed steer with a bullet in his neck.

Carberry drew his pistol, took aim at Jezebel's head from three feet away. Slocum swung his pistol toward

Carberry, and shot him twice, as fast as he could fan the hammer back.

Carberry's face exploded in blood as two bullets smashed into his mouth and nose. The bullets tore out the back of his head, sent chunks of skull flying. Carberry crumpled to the floor.

Jezebel screamed.

Slocum stooped down and jerked the fuse free of the cap, seconds before it would have exploded. The fuse burned the tip of his finger, but he didn't feel it. He dropped it to the floor, watched it fizzle out.

Jezebel looked up at him, then at the stick of dynamite in his hand.

"My God," she gasped, "that thing almost went off."

Slocum grinned as he helped her to her feet.

"Almost," he said.

He holstered his pistol, picked up his rifle. He put his arm around Jezebel's waist and led her to the door. They stepped over the two dead men and walked out onto the empty street together.

"Your pa's just fine," said Slocum. "Got a sore leg, but he'll live. He's at Mrs. Willoughby's."

"Oh, thank heavens," Jezebel exclaimed. "Then that must mean you met Amy Nichols."

"Yes."

"I see," said Jezebel, drooping her head.

He chucked her under the chin.

"No, you don't," he said.

"She is a beautiful woman. Living practically all alone in that big house."

"Yes, and so are you, Jezebel."

"Call me Jez," she said. "I'm grateful to you for saving my life and helping my pa."

"He would have done the same for me."

"And so would I," she said, her voice silky with promise.

They walked back toward Main, arm in arm. People rushed out from hiding, came up to Slocum, and slapped him on the back. Others poured into Carberry's office, surveyed the scene, and came out whooping with joy. Amy Nichols ran down the street toward Slocum and Jezebel as word of his victory spread like wildfire through the town.

Cheers rose up from a dozen voices. Amy threw her arms around Slocum's neck and peppered him with kisses. Then she released her grip and flung her arms around Jezebel, hugging her and kissing her on the cheeks.

Jezebel smiled, and tears came to her eyes.

"John Slocum," she said slowly, "you are a wicked man. But you are also wonderful."

"Yes," said Amy, "yes, he is. He truly is."

Slocum blushed as he put his arms around the waists of both women and walked in triumph toward the boarding house, the cheers ringing in his ears. Disappointed well-wishers fell away in his wake, stopped and stared after him.

Justice has been done, he thought, *and to the victor belongs the spoils.*

JAKE LOGAN